Camus's Récit *La Chute:*
A Rewriting Through Dante's *Commedia*

Studies in the Humanities

edited by
Guy Mermier

Vol. 5

PETER LANG
New York · Berne · Frankfurt am Main

Jacqueline Gabrielle Roston

Camus's Récit *La Chute* A Rewriting Through Dante's *Commedia*

PETER LANG
New York · Berne · Frankfurt am Main

Library of Congress Cataloging in Publication Data

Roston, Jacqueline Gabrielle
  Camus's Récit La Chute.

  (Studies in the Humanities; vol. 5)
  Bibliography: p.
  1. Camus, Albert, 1913–1960. Chute. 2. Dante
  Alighieri, 1265–1321. Divina commedia. I. Title.
  II. Series: Studies in the Humanities (New York, N.Y.)
  vol. 5.
  PQ2605.A3734C538   1986   843'.912   85-13182
  ISBN 0-8204-0269-9
  ISSN 0742-6712

CIP-Kurztitelaufnahme der Deutschen Bibliothek

Roston, Jacqueline Gabrielle:
Camus's Récit La Chute. A Rewriting Through
Dante's Commedia / Jacqueline Gabrielle Roston. –
New York; Berne; Frankfurt am Main: Lang, 1985.
  (Studies in the Humanities; Vol. 5)
  ISBN 0-8204-0269-9

NE: GT

© Peter Lang Publishing, Inc., New York 1985

All rights reserved.
Reprint or reproduction, even partially, in all forms such as
microfilm, xerography, microfiche, microcard, offset strictly prohibited.

Printed by Lang Druck, Inc., Liebefeld/Berne (Switzerland)

Table of Contents

	Page
Preface	iii
I. *La Chute* and Valéry's Poetics	1
II. Literal Distortions, the Hypothesis, and Foreshadows of the Coincidence	33
III. "Rewriting" the First Part of Clamence's Account: Suggestions and Concretions	49
IV. Isotopic Concretions and Assimilations	99
Conclusions	165
Bibliography	177

Preface

The study of literature as such seems to have great difficulty in establishing its own meaningful territory for practical purposes. In large part, this is due to the massive incompetence for which the field makes gracious allowances. Among its participants, I include those who have been given too much praise for having mastered a narrow vocabulary of some branch of literary philosophy or criticism, which they evasively tack on to the text of their choice. On the other end of the scale, there is always the person who precisely examines all facets of the definite article or the semiotics of a tapestry or painting and comes up with astounding conclusions, or, more precisely, with no conclusions at all. We seem to be becoming increasingly talented at verbalizing nothing, creating distinctions where there virtually are none, or at least none that have any consequence.

Gérard Genette, who aims to consider literature taken for itself, and not as a historical document, constructs a precise vocabulary to describe the various interacting successions into which he has decomposed the written work; but this process often ends up by being even more exterior to the text that the historical factor, which, after all, is engrained in it. In Genette's *Palimpsestes*,[1] his goals are clearly founded on what would seem to be perfect statement of the rewritten relationship between *La Chute* and the *Commedia*:

> L'objet de la poétique, disais-je à peu près,
> n'est pas le texte, considéré dans sa singula-
> rité (ceci est plutôt l'affaire de la critique),
> mais *l'architexte*, ou si l'on préfère l'archi-
> textualité du texte (comme on dit, et c'est
> à peu près la même chose, 'la littérarité de
> la littérature'), c'est à dire l'ensemble des
> catégories générales, ou transcendantes-types
> de discours, modes d'énonciation, genres lit-
> téraires, etc. dont relève chaque texte singu-
> lier. Je dirais plutôt aujourd'hui, plus large-
> ment, que cet objet est la transtextualité,
> ou transcendance textuelle du texte, que je
> définissais déjà, grossièrement, par 'tout ce
> qui le met en relation manifeste ou secrète,
> avec d'autres textes.[2]

Nowhere are we provided with the study of the true palimpsest, one which does not exist until we perceive the former or erased underlying text(s) of the parchment; and once again, we find ourselves outside the issue. Genette's palimpsests concern the sort of intertextuality and deviation requiring reader recognition of authorial intention; to transform for example, parody into a series of technically labelled stages really adds nothing to anyone's reading of a parody, or any other *détournements* examined in his study of "second degree" literature. It side-steps the issue. One must try to distinguish between the useful and the useless series of distinctions; the purpose is to bring something other to the literal level and to implicate this exterior element within the text, to prove that it actually functions to explain or engender the literal level and not to fabricate unnecessary divisions within a single term which already has precise meaning.

On the subject of "writing around"--that is, the *écrire*, we also seem inclined, these days, to examine the etymology of a word for several pages before we can legitimately use it. If the etymology is shown to be a part of the text's motivating forces, the process is entirely a different matter and a valid undertaking; but otherwise, why do we need to break words down before we can use them if we all know what they mean? We all know by now that the heart of the matter does not exist anyway; or, as Valéry words it in terms of this fascination with Narcissus:

> Ce que je puis de moins en moins comprendre, c'est qu'on puisse parler parler parler (écrire écrire écrire) tout à coup sur des faits particuliers sans s'arrêter d'abord - assez pour avoir envie d'*aller au fond*. Il n'y a pas de fond.[3]
> (*Cahiers*, p. 309)

Those of us, who are supposed to take literature as an object for study, have so often transformed it into an increasingly narcissistic activity; it is evident that so much of today's criticism takes itself for literature.

Almost all literary criticism depicts the written work as secondary, a historical document, the reenactment of a primordial scene, or any one of numerous marks other than itself. Obviously one does not want to deal purely with style or subject, unless one considers them to the point of mimesis and semiosis. But so often do we produce a summary, or a list sometimes followed by an enlightened remark. If anything, those of us associated with philosophy and the arts should have much more inventive thought required of us at the early stages of our apprenticeship to the field than those in the sciences, who, on the global scale, learn a routine and put

it to use in the office, laboratory, or computer; but since
the building blocks of literature are nothing one can memorize,
due to the fact that its terms remain undefined, it makes too
much room for ignorance and charm, defined by Camus's *juge-
pénitent* as:

> . . . une manière répondre oui sans avoir posé
> aucune question claire.
> (*La Chute*, p. 1504)

One thing remains certain; all good critical analysis
makes use of a double perspective. Even with respect to the
involution of the text itself, a broad overview of the course
of French literature reveals the tendency of writing to turn
more and more towards itself and an increasing destruction of
the links to the world we recognize. The process, marked by
continuity between the source and its reflection, is one of
self-continuity between the source and its reflection, is one
of self-destruction and self-purification. The double structure is the essence of the definitively undefinable term of
littérarité. The artistic concepts presented through the writings of Valéry and Proust so precisely focus upon the essen-
tial and all-encompassing nature of the narcissistic, metonymic, and metaphoric characteristics. At least in French literature, throughout all of its periods, the exploitation in
different directions of language and representation has structurally proven the presence of the "imitative" factor, whether
on the level of repeated structures, the imitation of reality,
the imitation of language, or of any other thinkable reflection; in fact, French literature of the sixteenth century

spells out the passage from imitation, to discovery, to involution. While reflection marks the *epistēmē* of that epoch, it certainly marks every other one as a well, even if the constituent elements of distortion and *déjouement* occur in different ways. As regards the *littérarité* of a text, one concludes that it is the *mise-en-scène* of the *penser:peser* relationship expression, and resulting tension on various levels which should concern every reader; or, perhaps in more precise terms, the elements of the same and the other, repetition, resemblance, imitation, reflection, duality, successions, irreversibility and reversibility, the finite and the infinite, energy and entropy and conservatoin, restitution or recuperative function, weight and thought, transformations, equilibrium, distortions, and in fact all of those recurrent elements of Valery's *Cahiers*, which find themselves put to use in his poetry. These are also the very same elements which so centrally concern various readings of Proust and find themselves so very concretely synthesized in a discussion of metaphor and metonymy. This example is of course too well chosen, but that makes no difference, for these are still the terms through which one can approach any piece of literature and draw conclusions upon its artistic concepts and its literary quality, whether these terms are self-contained within the object of our reading, or introduced into it by the terms against which we may choose to approach it.

It is clear that the rewriting as which I present Albert Camus's *La Chute* proposes a new dimension to the meaning of *littérarité* and to intertextuality--new insofar as its relationship to the above elements has never before been shown to function on that particular level of a true palimpsest, one which does not exist until the reader perceives it, anticipates further precision regarding it, and repeatedly finds *La Chute*'s own coherence to confirm the presence of the *Commedia* as valid. If one takes the production of the literal level to be the object of analysis, then structural models such as those provided by social codes, history, psychoanalysis, biology, calculus, thermodynamics, the text itself, and so many others are clear signs of the text's *littérarité*; but specifically is not a characteristic of such "imitation." The point to which *La Chute* implicates *The Divine Comedy* is the mark of outstanding literary value and further proof that a consciousness of the terms of Valéry's poetics can lead to the discovery (or uncovering) of important textual dimensions.

Authorial intent is of no issue in the following study, but certainly we have every right to assume that an educated person, especially of Camus's generation, was familiar with Dante's *Commedia*; therefore, I never mean to imply that the Dantesque presence conferred upon the *récit* by rewriting materializes out of nowhere, particularly since the specificity is often so striking.

I also want to emphasize the fact that I never mean to account for the whole coherence of *La Chute* through the rewriting. Conclusive proof of the Dantesque underlying force comes to exist through the study of limited passages. Most thoroughly examined is the first portion of the *récit* from beginning to end; this is because I wish to convey step by step how the rewriting should be read; also, the rewriting process of this first portion occurs in a densely exemplary fashion as well as presenting numerous clues to be followed through the remainder of Clamence's *récit*. The most interesting specificity occurs in latter less densely rewritten portions of the text. Furthermore, repetition of a language which could be taken as situated somewhere on the path to the identification of the Dantesque presence finds itself in great abundance throughout the text, and it serves really no purpose to repeat such intermediate examples with respect to the examination of the motivational force. One just makes a note of their mass and general existence. This study concerns itself most with the passage from hint to precision, one might say from intertextuality to isotope, and makes use of the tools of context or contiguity, repetition, length or mass, density, and specificity for the discernment of the Dantesque presence.

Footnotes to Preface

[1] Gérard Genette, *Palimpsestes* (Paris: Seuil, collection Poétique, 1982), pp. 11-12.

[2] Ibid., p. 7.

[3] All references to and citations from the notebooks follow the text established by the Centre National de la Recherche Scientifique, *Cahiers*, of Paul Valéry (Paris: Centre National de la Recherche Scientifique, Vol. II, 1957).

[4] All references to and citations from the *récit* follow the text established by Roger Quillot, *Théâtre, récits, nouvelles*, of Albert Camus (Paris: Gallimard, Bibliothèque de la Pléiade, 1962), pp. 1477-1551.

I.

La Chute and Valéry's Poetics

Before beginning the examination of *La Chute* with relationship to the *Commedia,* let us consider the coherence of Camus's *récit* with respect to the artistic concepts presented through Valéry's *Cahiers* (and supported by his poetry), since I am considering these poetic elements as constituting a clear statement of the fundamental terms of literary quality.

> Tout ce qui arrive à l'esprit le conduit hors
> de cette chose qui lui arrive. Mais il peut
> s'y ramener.
> (*Cahiers*, p. 243)

Within the natural series, the mind is clearly powerless. It is only through the reflective action of *s'y ramener* that it is able to recuperate something. The *je* must attempt to lead an imitation of the natural series--an imitation which results in the game that allows the *je* to preserve something.

> Même quand je suis certain qu'une chose est
> ceci, je puis même <u>être contraint</u> de l'imaginer
> <u>autre</u>. . . . La certitude vient de l'assimila-
> tion d'une chose à une autre chose à l'égard
> de laquelle notre impuissance est continuelle-
> ment éprouvée.
> (*Cahiers*, p. 338)

As the *Cahiers* often insist upon the fact that *les corps sont pesants* and upon the relationship *penser:peser,* our power to weigh something is also the power to think it--that is, to fabricate a series of relationships that produce it. Jean-Baptiste's power is the same:

> Qu'importait le mensonge d'un homme dans l'his-
> toire des générations et quelle prétention de
> vouloir amener dans la lumière de la vérité

> une misérable tromperie, perdue dans l'océan
> des âges comme le grain de sel dans la mer!
> (*La Chute*, p. 1521)

As *La Chute* recounts a conversion, the correction to Jean-Baptiste's former upstanding and harmonious life can be envisioned entirely as his ability to create and perceive forms that contain. For Valéry, the whole imitative process is based upon the principle that consciousness enters into a relationship of energy exchange with the object of its awareness:

> On suit ce qui contient.
> (*Cahiers*, p. 241)

Nature's continuity knows no definitive difference, time, or death while the prolongations of art introduce discontinuity and mark time:

> Toutes les fois que l'imagination tend à s'effectuer sur un système de signes (c.à.d. à imaginer une représentation) tout phénomène peut être divisé de sorte que chaque partie γ soit signifiable. Dans cette transformation le temps intervient. De plus il faut que cette transformation conserve quelque chose.
> (*Cahiers*, p. 254)

The energy level of art necessarily exists at a higher level than that of nature, and Valéry stresses the "power" once again:

> Notre pouvoir est dans l'interruption systématique qui transforme une question jusqu'à un certain état où . . . le régime reprend.
> (*Cahiers*, p. 316)

To "créer en images une sorte de durée imitée de la durée physique" (*Cahiers*, p. 296), means that the artificial series created through difference must imitate resemblance or the fact that two naturally successive elements can actually be reduced to the *same*.

> Le secret des transformations échappe car en décomposant deux choses, on trouve de préten-
> dues notions communes aux deux qui impliquent déjà la transformation
> (*Cahiers*, p. 295)

The resemblance factor is natural. A powerful imitation can provide metonymy and narcissism, both highly recurrent in Valéry's poetry and essentially based upon irreducible difference as well as the link of resemblance.

> Les choses qui se suivent s'éteignent à mesure par le tout ancien. Alors l'art cherche à remplacer leur destruction fatale par leur suppression voulue en mettant après chacune telle autre chose assez rapprochée pour se mêler au retentissement de la première formant avec elle une nouvelle chose assez déterminée qui se substitue entièrement à ses composantes.
> (*Cahiers*, p. 250)

The power of art is to "feindre des obstacles," the "rapprochement de choses sans unité interne" (*Cahiers*, p. 274), since "le concept commun les annullerait" (*Cahiers*, p. 273), and to give "l'impression d'être mené là où l'écoulé sera saisi et possédé" (*Cahiers*, p. 250); *Le Cimetière marin*'s "creux toujours futur" and *Ebauche d'un serpent*'s "venir sans venir" are found again in the final words of *La Chute*:

> Cette étrange affection que je sentais pour vous avait donc du sens. Vous exercez à Paris la belle profession d'avocat! Je savais bien que nous étions de la même race. Ne sommes-nous pas tous semblables, parlant sans trêve et à personne, confrontés toujours aux mêmes questions bien que nous connaissions d'avance les réponses? Alors, racontez-moi, je vous prie, ce qui vous est arrivé un soir sur les quais de la Seine et comment vous avez réussi

> à ne jamais risquer votre vie. Prononcez vous-
> même les mots qui, depuis des années, n'ont
> cessé de retentir dans mes nuits, et que je
> dirai enfin par votre bouche: "O jeune fille,
> jette-toi encore dans l'eau pour que j'aie une
> seconde fois la chance de nous sauver tous les
> deux!" Une seconde fois, hein, quelle impru-
> dence! Supposez, cher maître, qu'on nous prenne
> au mot? Il faudrait s'exécuter. Brr...! l'eau
> est si froide! Mais rassurons-nous! Il est
> trop tard, maintenant, il sera toujours trop
> tard. Heureusement!
>
> (*La Chute*, p. 1551)

The extended use of the future tense, the fact of everything being already contained within everything else, the verbal illusion of having become *other,* and even the river and the plunge--all establish a crisis of narcissism, immobility, and continuity, and these are recurrent elements of Jean-Baptiste's true state, apparent in both past and present periods of his life. The present is really only a perfected vision of the past:

> Ce n'était pas facile; j'ai longtemps erré. Il
> a fallu d'abord que ce rire perpétuel, et les
> rieurs, m'apprissent à voir plus clair en moi,
> à découvrir enfin que je n'étais pas simple.
> Ne souriez pas, cette vérité n'est pas aussi
> première qu'elle paraît. On appelle vérités
> premières celles qu'on découvre après toutes
> les autres, voilà tout.
>
> (*La Chute*, p. 1518)

Departures must be expressed, but they must never reach their destination. They must only defer. The imitation of continuity must avoid equilibrium $\Delta = 0$. To avoid the zero is a mathematical lie, since the continuity of a function is based upon difference eventually becoming zero. In the passage quoted below, the "secret" is that moment of $\Delta = 0$; Jean-Baptiste will eventually contrive a means for preserving "secrets" as well as the "prétention de vouloir amener dans la vérité une misérable tromperie, perdue dans l'océan des des âges . . ." which will literally depict all the objects of the *récit*'s present point of view as they call him off course--even a black dot over the ocean (*La Chute*, p. 1539); however, the "secret" below lies within the $\Delta = 0$ of continuity which does not preserve anything:

> Parfois, tard dans ces nuits où la danse, l'alcool léger, mon déchaînement, le violent abandon de chacun, me jetaient dans un ravissement à la fois las et comblé il me semblait, à l'extrémité de la fatigue, et l'espace d'une seconde, que je comprenais enfin le secret des êtres et du monde. Mais la fatigue disparaissait le lendemain et, avec elle, le secret; je m'élançais de nouveau. Je courais ainsi toujours comblé, jamais rassasié, sans savoir où m'arrêter, jusqu'au jour, jusqu'au soir plutôt où la musique s'est arrêtée, les lumières se sont éteintes.
> (*La Chute*, pp. 1490-91)

Consciousness can never truthfully attain such a state: "l'équilibre $\Delta = 0$ est impossible et c'est la raison de la self-variance--nous connaissons "(*Cahiers*, p. 326), so Clamence's lie, the continuity which is actually immobility, imitates the lack of change inherent to continuity, and it remains true to consciousness in so doing. Even the mathematical concept of continuity is based upon an impossibility--the conceptual impossibility of difference eventually becoming zero:

> Les mensonges ne mettent-ils pas finalement sur la voie de la vérité? Et mes histoires, vraies ou fausses, ne tendent-elles pas toutes à la même fin, n'ont elles pas le même sens? Alors, qu'importe qu'elles soient vraies ou

> fausses si, dans les deux cas, elles sont significatives de ce que j'ai été et de ce que je suis.
> (*La Chute*, p. 1537)

Continuity succeeds in resembling immobility, and either way the result is fatal for the objects involved:

> La notion d'énergie permet de penser avec rigueur les transformations et conduit de façon à indiquer le sens général des transformations et la forme fatale où toutes les formes d'énergie tombent peu à peu.
> (*Cahiers*, p. 323)

Jean-Baptiste's *pouvoir* is in the deferal--that is, as long as it lasts:

> [J]e ne peux différer plus longtemps le récit [de cette aventure], malgré mes digressions et les efforts d'une invention à laquelle, je l'espère, vous rendez justice.
> (*La Chute*, p. 1510)

As the "brusque volte-face" (the conversion) of Clamence's life brings him to view even his past life as containing evidence towards the truthful realization of himself, it is no wonder that he becomes increasingly self-centered and preoccupied with being physically self-contained and self-confining, as he fights the tendency towards highest entropy.

> Oh! Avez-vous bien fermé la porte? Oui. Vérifiez, s'il vous plaît. Pardonnez-moi, j'ai le complexe du verrou. Au moment de m'endormir, je ne puis jamais savoir si j'ai poussé le verrou. Chaque soir, je dois me lever pour le vérifier. On n'est sûr de rien, je vous l'ai dit. Ne croyez pas que cette inquiétude du verrou soit chez moi une réaction de propriétaire apeuré. Autrefois, je ne fermais pas mon appartement à clé, ni ma voiture. Je ne serrais pas mon argent, je ne tenais pas à ce que je possédais. A vrai dire, j'avais un peu honte de posséder. Ne m'arrivait-il pas, dans mes discours mondains, de m'écrier avec conviction: "La propriété, messieurs, c'est le meurtre!" N'ayant pas le cœur assez grand

> pour partager mes richesses avec un pauvre bien
> méritant, je les laissais à la disposition des
> voleurs éventuels, espérant ainsi corriger l'in-
> justice par le hasard. Aujourd'hui, du reste,
> je ne possède rien. Je ne m'inquiète donc pas
> de ma sécurité, mais de moi-même et de ma pré-
> sence d'esprit. Je tiens aussi à condamner
> la porte du petit univers bien clos dont je
> suis le roi, le pape et le juge.
> (La Chute, p. 1541)

With his awareness, he even grew fatter:

> Je grossissais un peu. . . .
> (La Chute, p. 1530)

The terms of conservation, perservation, and immortality enter his thoughts to an obsessional point; fullness, emptiness, openings, closures, lies and secrets also prove themselves to be the often motivating forces behind these terms:

> Je suis bavard, hélas! Et me lie facilement.
> Bien que je sache garder les distances qui con-
> viennent, toutes les occasions sont bonnes.
> (La Chute, p. 1478)

> Voyez, par exemple, au-dessus de sa tête, sur
> le mur de fond, ce rectangle vide qui marque
> la place d'un tableau décroché.
> (La Chute, p. 1478)

> Enfin, je vous amuse, ce qui, sans vanité, sup-
> pose chez vous une certaine ouverture d'esprit.
> (La Chute, p. 1480)

> Mais c'est le trop-plein; dès que j'ouvre la
> bouche, les phrases coulent. Ce pays m'inspire,
> d'ailleurs. J'aime ce peuple, grouillant sur
> les trottoirs, coincé dans un petit espace de
> maisons et d'eaux, cerné par des brumes, des
> terres froides, et la mer fumante comme une
> lessive. Je l'aime, car il est double. Il
> est ici et il est ailleurs.
> (La Chute, p. 1482)

> Je ne passe jamais sur un pont, la nuit. C'est
> la conséquence d'un voeu.
> (La Chute, p. 1483)

Ces dames, derrière ces vitrines? Le rêve, monsieur, le rêve à peu de frais, le voyage aux Indes! Ces personnes se parfument aux épices. Vous entrez, elles tirent les rideaux et la navigation commence. Les dieux descendent sur les corps nus et les îles dérivent, démentes, coiffées d'une chevelure ébouriffée de palmiers sous le vent. Essayez.
(*La Chute*, p. 1483)

Le ciel nous préserve, cher monsieur, d'être placés trop haut par nos amis.
(*La Chute*, p. 1491)

Je sentais monter en moi un vaste sentiment de puissance et, comment dirais-je, d'achèvement, qui dilatait mon coeur.
(*La Chute*, p.1495)

Mais ce soir, non plus, je ne me sens pas en forme. J'ai même du mal à tourner mes phrases. Je parle moins bien, il me semble, et mon discours est moins sûr. Le temps, sans doute. On respire mal, l'air est si lourd qu'il pèse sur la poitrine. Verriez-vous un inconvénient, mon cher compatriote, à ce que nos sortions pour marcher un peu dans la ville? Merci.
(*La Chute*, p. 1497)

J'ai toujours crevé de vanité. Moi, moi moi, voilà le refrain de ma chère vie, et qui s'entendait dans tout ce que je disais.
(*La Chute*, p. 1500)

Il [le ciel] s'épaissit, puis se creuse, ouvre des escaliers d'air, ferme la porte des nuées.
(*La Chute*, p. 1512)

Sans doute, me soupçonnaient-ils de vivre pleinement et dans un libre abandon. . . .
(*La Chute*, p. 1516)

J'étais comme mes Hollandais qui sont là sans y être; absent au moment où je tenais le plus de place.
(*La Chute*, p. 1520)

Je mesurais les années qui me séparaient de ma fin.
(*La Chute*, p. 1521)

Comme, à l'état de veille, et pour peu qu'on se connaisse, on n'aperçoit pas de raisons

> valables pour que l'immortalité soit conférée à
> un singe salace, il faut bien se procurer des
> succédanés de cette immortalité. Parce que
> je désirais la vie éternelle, je couchais donc
> avec des putains et je buvais pendant des nuits.
> Le matin, bien sûr, j'avais dans la bouche le
> goût amer de la condition mortelle. Mais,
> pendant de longues heures, j'avais plané, bien-
> heureux. Oserais-je vous l'avouer?
> (*La Chute*, p. 1528)

> Mais j'ai bu l'eau, cela est sûr, en me persua-
> dant que les autres avaient besoin de moi, plus
> que de celui qui devait mourir de toute façon,
> et je devais me conserver à eux.
> (*La Chute*, p. 1541)

> Ouvrez un peu la fenêtre, je vous prie, il fait
> ici une chaleur extraordinaire. Pas trop, car
> j'ai froid aussi. Mon idée est à la fois sim-
> ple et féconde. Comment mettre tout le monde
> dans le bain pour avoir le droit de se sécher
> soi-même au soleil?
> (*La Chute*, p. 1546)

The above examples express Clamence's obsession with an almost mathematical exchange (further supported by his geometrical allusions to horizontal and vertical lines, circles, degrees, order, arrangements, and continuity) ultimately seeking to refuse natural order through the power to maintain difference and resemblance and to contain.

> Quand je m'occupais d'autrui, c'était pure con-
> descendance, en toute liberté, et le mérite
> entier m'en revenait: je montais d'un degré
> dans l'amour que je me portais.
> Avec quelques autres vérités, j'ai découvert
> ces évidences peu à peu, dans la période qui
> suivit le soir dont je vous ai parlé. Pas tout
> de suite, non, ni très distinctement. Il a
> fallu d'abord que je retrouve la mémoire. Par
> degrés, j'ai vu plus clair, j'ai appris un
> peu de ce que je savais. Jusque-là, j'avais
> toujours été aidé par un étonnant pouvoir
> d'oubli. J'oubliais tout, et d'abord mes ré-
> solutions. Au fond, rien ne comptait.
> (*La Chute*, p. 1500)

The pervading role of "memory" is a necessary step in the linking process:

> [L]e souvenir tend vers l'imitation. . . .
> (*Cahiers*, p. 294)

Everywhere, Jean-Baptiste's desire to be "here and elsewhere" (*same* and *other*) is made evident. Resemblance and memory must recuperate respectively difference and *oubli,* the latter in which he explicitly corrects the expression of himself from object to subject:

> [J]e fabrique un portrait qui est celui de tous et de personne. [L]e portrait que je tends à mes contemporains devient un miroir.
> (*La Chute*, p. 1547)

> Peu à peu, la mémoire m'est cependant revenue. Ou plutôt je suis revenu à elle, et j'y ai trouvé le souvenir qui m'attendait.
> (*La Chute*, p. 1500)

Jean-Baptiste also progressively assimilates the language he has used to perceive the exterior. Examples of words that pass from the third to the first person (and most often to the reflexive or pronominal) include *coincé, coucher, couper, coller, coller, errer, dériver, glisser, trôner,* and even such details as the *cendres*:

> A notre gauche, ce tas de cendres qu'on appelle ici une dune, la digue grise à notre droite, la grève livide à nos pieds et, devant nous, la mer couleur de lessive faible, le vaste ciel où se reflètent les eaux blêmes.
> (*La Chute*, p. 1512)

> Couvert de cendres, m'arrachant lentement les cheveux, le visage labouré par les ongles, mais le regard perçant, je me tiens devant l'humanité entière. . . .
> (*La Chute*, p. 1547)

The same ability to reflect the exterior occurs in regard to duplicity, insanity, the giving up of worldly goods, the fact of being a prophet, the *diable,* the fact of "taking literally," the circle and line, suspicion, flight, confinement, decapitation, the synecdochical *têtes* and *bouches*, loss of boats, the theft of the painting, the plunge, the corps, the laughter, the cry, and the bent over form, initially apparent in the woman who threw herself over the bridge. Her "forme penchée" of which one only saw the "nuque fraîche et mouillée" is suggested near the end of the *récit*:

> Tous réunis, enfin, mais à genoux, et la tête courbée.
> (*La Chute*, p. 1545)

Along with increasing expression of mirror images or reflections, paradox, and miracles, the fact of the above evidence lying within the progress of the *récit*'s diegesis proves the fight against time as carried out by words. The increasing power to contain is necessarily accompanied by the power to realize splits on a multitude of levels, and Amsterdam has provided the necessary terms of this narcissistic continuity from which to create an imitation. The "venir sans venir" is perfectly synthesized and finally stated in the present time frame:

> Nous avançons et rien ne change.
> (*La Chute*, p. 1525)

To depart without arriving anywhere has become the rule of Clamence's life, but the consciousness of immobility is the price he eventually must pay--once again, as before:

> Supposez, après tout, que quelqu'un se jette à l'eau.
> (*La Chute*, p. 1483)
>
> Il faut que quelque chose arrive. . . .
> (*La Chute*, p. 1494)
>
> Que faire pour être un autre? Impossible.
> (*La Chute*, p. 1550)
>
> Il faut tout de même que je sorte.
> (*La Chute*, p. 1550)

The supposition that the doves do finally descend, that the snow actually catches fire, that Clamence is decapitated, that he becomes *other* and that he will plunge--all concretize the hysteria of desired and negated movement, conveniently put off to the future. The necessity to change without changing and the elements inherent to this process make themselves evident in the episode of laughter which sets off the conversion to the present state:

> J'étais monté sur le pont des Arts, désert à cette heure, pour regarder le fleuve qu'on devinait à peine dans la nuit maintenant venue. Face au Vert-Galant, je dominais l'île. Je sentais monter en moi un vaste sentiment de puissance et, comment dirais-je, d'achèvement, qui dilatait mon cœur. Je me redressai et j'allais allumer une cigarette, la cigarette de la satisfaction, quand, au même moment, un rire éclata derrière moi. Surpris, je fis une brusque volte-face: il n'y avait personne. J'allai jusqu'au garde-fou: aucune péniche, aucune barque. Je me retournai vers l'île et, de nouveau, j'entendis le rire dans mon dos, un peu plus lointain, comme s'il descendait le fleuve. Je restais là, immobile. Le rire décroissait, mais je l'entendais encore distinctement derrière moi, venu de nulle part, sinon des eaux. En même temps, je percevais les battements précipités de mon cœur. Entendez-moi bien, ce rire n'avait rien de mystérieux, c'était un bon rire, naturel, presque amical, qui remettait les choses en place. Bientôt d'ailleurs, je n'entendis plus rien. Je regagnai les quais, pris la rue Dauphine,

> achetai des cigarettes dont je n'avais nul besoin. J'étais étourdi, je respirais mal. Ce soir-là, j'appelai un ami qui n'était pas chez lui. J'hésitais à sortir, quand, soudain, j'entendis rire sous mes fenêtres. J'ouvris. Sur le trottoir, en effet, des jeunes gens se séparaient joyeusement. Je refermai les fenêtres en haussant les épaules; après tout, j'avais un dossier à étudier. Je me rendis dans la salle de bains pour boire un verre d'eau. Mon image souriait dans la glace, mais il me sembla que mon sourire était double...
> (*La Chute*, p. 1495)

The laughter seems to come from the water, follows Clamence home to "outside" his window. It is a call to the exterior which he has ignored until then, seeming to move away from him downstream. People and boats are absent. Clamence phones a friend who is not home. People on the street "separate." All of these perceptions point to an emphasis on departure and the inability to reach the next point in the succession. The above passage is also a concise statement of Jean-Baptiste's physical self-confinement and self-containment, immobility, reflection in the mirror, duplicity, hesitation, and final drink of water--all imitating the narcissistic solution.

The recovered memory of the woman who threw herself over the bridge structurally contains those same elements again:

> Cette nuit-là, en novembre, deux ou trois ans avant le soir où je crus entendre rire dans mon dos, je regagnais la rive gauche, et mon domicile, par le pont Royal. Il était une heure après minuit, une petite pluie tombait, une bruine plutôt, qui dispersait les rares passants. Je venais de quitter une amie qui, surement, dormait déjà. J'étais heureux de cette marche, un peu engourdi, le corps calmé, irrigué par un sang doux comme la pluie qui tombait. Sur le pont, je passai derrière une forme penchée sur le parapet, et qui semblait

> regarder le fleuve. De plus près, je distinguai
> une mince jeune femme, habillée de noir. Entre
> les cheveux sombres et le col du manteau, on
> voyait seulement une nuque, fraîche et mouillée,
> à laquelle je fus sensible. Mais je poursuivis
> ma route, après une hésitation. Au bout du
> pont, je pris les quais en direction de Saint-
> Michel, où je demeurais. J'avais déjà parcouru
> une cinquantaine de mètres à peu près, lorsque
> j'entendis le bruit, qui, malgré la distance,
> me parut formidable dans le silence nocturne,
> d'un corps qui s'abat sur l'eau. Je m'arrêtai
> net, mais sans me retourner. Presque aussitôt,
> j'entendis un cri, plusieurs fois répété, qui
> descendait lui aussi le fleuve, puis s'éteignit
> brusquement. Le silence qui suivit, dans la
> nuit soudain figée, me parut interminable.
> Je voulus courir et je ne bougeai pas. Je trem-
> blais, je crois, de froid et de saisissement.
> Je me disais qu'il fallait faire vite et je
> sentais une faiblesse irrésistible envahir mon
> corps. J'ai oublié ce que j'ai pensé alors.
> "Trop tard, trop loin..." ou quelque chose de
> ce genre. J'écoutais toujours, immobile. Puis
> à petits pas, sous la pluie, je m'éloignai.
> Je ne prévins personne.
>
> (*La Chute*, p. 1511)

Silence, immobility, separations, and distances direct this conversion incident. The "hésitation" and "entre" are narcissistic elements that present themselves once again. It is no surprise that this original of the conversion incidents presents a call to the *other*, moving away from Clamence "downstream." Likewise for the *corps* that fills, the "turning around," the night, the sense of infinity or no change or continuity, the wish for movement that finds itself immobile, and the eventual isolation or removal from the exterior. The black dot Clamence once sighted over the ocean and the present cry of gulls provide the same structural continuity:

> Un jour pourtant, au cours d'un voyage que
> j'offris à une amie, sans lui dire que je le
> faisais pour fêter ma guérison, je me trouvais

> à bord d'un transatlantique, sur le pont supé-
> rieur, naturellement. Soudain, j'aperçus au large
> un point noir sur l'océan couleur de fer. Je
> détournai les yeux aussitôt, mon cœur se mit
> à battre. Quand je me forçai à regarder, le
> point noir avait disparu. J'allais crier, ap-
> peler stupidement à l'aide, quand je le revis.
> Il s'agissait d'un de ces débris que les navires
> laissent derrière eux. Pourtant, je n'avais
> pu supporter de le regarder, j'avais tout de
> suite pensé à un noyé. Je compris alors, sans
> révolte, comme on se résigne à une idée dont
> on connaît depuis longtemps la vérité, que ce
> cri qui, des années auparavant, avait retenti
> sur la Seine, derrière moi, n'avait pas cessé,
> porté par le fleuve vers les eaux de la Manche,
> de cheminer dans le monde, à travers l'étendue
> illimitée de l'océan, et qu'il m'y avait attendu
> jusqu'à ce jour où je l'avais rencontré. Je
> compris aussi qu'il continuerait de m'attendre
> sur les mers et les fleuves, partout enfin où
> se trouverait l'eau amère de mon baptême. Ici
> encore, dites-moi, ne sommes-nous pas sur l'eau?
> Sur l'eau plate, monotone, interminable, qui
> confond ses limites à celles de la terre? Com-
> ment croire que nous allons arriver à Amsterdam?
> Nous ne sortirons jamais de ce bénitier immense.
> Ecoutez! N'entendez-vous pas les cris de goé-
> lands invisibles? S'ils crient vers nous, à
> quoi donc nous appellent-ils?
>   Mais ce sont les mêmes qui criaient, qui
> appelaient déjà sur l'Atlantique, le jour où
> je compris définitivement que je n'étais pas
> guéri, que j'étais toujours coincé, et qu'il
> fallait m'en arranger. Finie la vie glorieuse,
> mais finis aussi la rage et les soubresauts.
> Il fallait se soumettre et reconnaître sa cul-
> pabilité. Il fallait vivre dans le malconfort.
> C'est vrai, vous ne connaissez pas cette cel-
> lule de basse-fosse qu'au Moyen Age on appelait
> le malconfort.
>
>   (*La Chute*, pp. 1530-1531)

Immobility is once again apparent in the fact of sighting some-

thing and turning away, creating a sort of Gorgon incident.

The "turning around," the immobility, the call towards some-

thing that moves away or disappears, the water, and continu-

ity--all are elements of Clamence's perceptions that represent the truth of consciousness. Throughout his *récit*, and particularly in Amsterdam (the present), the excessive sirens, the search for shores and other signs which vanish from sight, confinement, and a dreamlike lack of movement dictate Clamence's point of view and transform his vision of the past so as to perfect his narcissism. Deferal establishes itself once again as the rule of his life.

As the order of his new life has consciously reintroduced the necessity not to arrive at a destination, while raising the "contained" energy level of forms and maintaining the illusion of movement as long as possible, Jean-Baptiste must break the contrived continuity at calculated moments:

> [B]aiser la main d'une pauvre femme et briser là, croyez moi, cher monsieur, c'est atteindre plus haut que l'ambitieux vulgaire et se hisser à ce point culminant où la vertu ne se nourrit plus que d'elle-même.
> (*La Chute*, p. 1487)

> Tous ces livres à peine lus, ces amis à peine aimés, ces villes à peine visitées, ces femmes à peine prises! Je faisais des gestes par ennui, ou par distraction. Les êtres suivaient, ils voulaient s'accrocher, mais il n'y avait rien, et c'était le malheur. Pour eux. Car, pour moi, j'oubliais, Je ne me suis jamais souvenu que de moi-même.
> (*La Chute*, p. 1501)

> Je l'abandonnais et la reprenais, la forçais à se donner dans des temps et des lieux qui ne s'y prêtaient pas, la traitais de façon si brutale, dans tous les domaines, que je finis par m'attacher à elle comme j'imagine que le geôlier se lie à son prisonnier. Et cela jusqu'au jour où, dans le violent désordre d'un plaisir douloureux et contraint, elle rendit hommage à voix haute à ce qui l'asservissait. Ce jour-là je commencai à m'éloigner d'elle. Depuis, je l'ai oubliée.
> (*La Chute*, p. 1508)

> [I]l s'agit de couper au jugement. . . . Pour
> la puissance bien sûr.
> <div align="right">(<i>La Chute</i>, p. 1517)</div>
>
> L'idée, par exemple, que je suis seul à connaître ce que tout le monde cherche et que j'ai chez moi un objet qui a fait courir en vain trois polices est purement délicieuse.
> <div align="right">(<i>La Chute</i>, p. 1521)</div>
>
> [N]ous sommes dans l'ordre. La justice étant définitivement séparée de l'innocence . . . j'ai le champ libre pour travailler selon mes convictions.
> <div align="right">(<i>La Chute</i>, p. 1542-1543)</div>
>
> J'ai découvert qu'en attendant la venue des maîtres et de leurs verges, nous devions, comme Copernic, inverser le raisonnement pour triompher. . . . [I]l fallait prendre la route en sens inverse. . . . Vous me suivez?
> <div align="right">(<i>La Chute</i>, p. 1546)</div>

Similarly, the "circle of which Jean-Baptiste was the center broke and they all lined up" (*La Chute*, p. 1515), the search for desert islands is impossible since "there are no longer any left" (*La Chute*, p. 1526), and the gods and doves of the *récit* are constantly looking for a place to land.

On another level, the separation is realized in the passage from figurative to literal meaning, which most often coincides with the passage from the third to the first person of the *récit*. The *errer, s'égarer*, and so many forms of flight throughout the text are accompanied by the high frequency of *(s)'arrêter*. The use of the *coeur* arrives at the expression of the "center of the Earth" (*La Chute*, p. 1483); the *couper au jugement* formula arrives at a razor cut (*La Chute*, p. 1515) and at a decapitation (*La Chute*, p. 1550); the *coincé* arrives at the fact of being physically "stuck" (*La Chute*, p. 1531), and the *coller* finds itself used to attach two people literally together. The frequent usage of the *enseignes*, the *servitude*, the *cellule*, and the terms of bondage, classification, and condemnation--all have the same containing and binding effect. The passage from Clamence's expression of dream to reality (or the realistic evocation) does the same thing. Likewise, the insistance of repetition contributes to the process. The figurative and frequent use of a vocabulary that designates altitudes also turns into a deformative reality, and Jean-Baptiste admits it:

> Je visais plus haut; vous verrez que l'expression est exacte en ce qui me concerne.
> (*La Chute*, p. 1485)

Even though islands have no figurative meaning, their first occurrence (*La Chute*, p. 1483) is part of a dream, but when Jean-Baptiste starts bringing them again and again into the subject of conversation they eventually acquire a physical meaning. The same thing occurs in regard to the *sirènes* of the *récit*. The *bouches* and *têtes* of the *récit* also fall into the expression of literal splits. Likewise for the exclamatory *Diable* and *l'enfer*. The locusts of the *récit* also engender a deformation: Their first occurrence is as follows:

> [J]'admettais les sauterelles.
> (*La Chute*, p. 1484)

The statement, which could have been taken in passing as an intertextual reference suprisingly finds itself followed by an extensive deformation:

> Avec la différence que les invasions de les or-
> thoptères ne m'ont jamais rapporté un cen-
> time. . . .
> (*La Chute*, p. 1485)

The Medieval suggestion of Clamence's past and emphasized *géné-rosité* and *courtoisie* finds the explicit reference to the Middle Ages in the recurring reference to Isolda's love and finally:

> Il fallait vivre dans le malconfort. C'est
> vrai, vous ne connaissez pas cette cellule de
> basse-fosse qu'au Moyen Age on appelait le mal-
> confort.
> (*La Chute*, 1531)

And the strong suggestion of Dante in the "concentric circles" and accompanying elements (p. 1483) does the same thing:

> Connaissez-vous Dante? Vraiment? Diable.
> Vous savez donc que Dante admet des anges neu-
> tres dans la querelle entre Dieu et Satan.
> Et il les place dans les Limbes, une sorte de
> vestibule de son enfer. Nous sommes dans le
> vestibule, cher ami.
> (*La Chute*, p. 1518)

The recurrent *fond, liens, sens, détourner, trancher, glisser,* reflexivity, figurative departures, *peser* and *poids*, rumination, and *objects* of the *récit* also succeed in detaching themselves from the continuity of natural expression. There are countless examples of the process. And one should also include, among these departures, the events of Clamence's life that find the means to take on heroic, mythological and other inhuman attributes; the inevitability of this movement is clearly related to insanity and/or death, and the repetition of such language or the length of such descriptions supports the distortion all the more. In the final paragraph of the *récit*, the literal meaning of words comes into play explicitly, once again, and its juxtaposition to "execution" confirms its role (and the literal echoes send us back to the first part of the *récit*, just as the often metonymic, burst, and final images of Valéry's poems send us back to an initial metaphor):

> Supposez, cher maître, qu'on nous prenne au mot? Il faudrait s'exécuter.
> (*La Chute*, p. 1551)

The literal deformation does in fact dictate a split. The final need to open windows, desire to leave, visions, decapitation, expression of miracles, and paradox are all fatal marks of the process, which literally gives "weight" back to the objects of expression.

As we talk about such extensive energy filled forms, let us now examine the role of light, since it leads the game of natural continuity, opening its forms to equilibrium $\Delta = 0$:

> Ce que nous désirons le plus ce sont, les images de lumière, de mouvement, de tension, la faculté de pouvoir tenir une chose pour un degré de son espèce.
> (*Cahiers*, p. 276)

The light of the natural series is a consuming one, realizing or opening its objects to their "forme fatale." As Clamence's second life or state of narcissism was self-induced, a conscious realization of the lie true to consciousness, one expects the loss of direct light, the omnipresence of night, and the presence of empty or glowing forms. His former life, maintaining the fire of himself only, reveals a light that victimized him, produced him, inflated him, and dehumanized him, and he insists on the *nature* and *naturel* throughout, contrary to the nature of human consciousness:

> Un balcon naturel, à cinq ou six cents mètres
> au-dessus d'une mer encore visible et baignée
> de lumière, était au contraire l'endroit où
> je respirais le mieux, surtout si j'étais seul,
> bien au-dessus des fourmis humaines. . . . [L]es
> miracles de feu se fissent sur des hauteurs
> accessbles. . . . Je grimpais sur la hauteur,
> j'y allumais des feux apparents, et une joyeuse
> salutation s'élevait vers moi.
> (*La Chute*, p. 1488)

As he is filled with light and in harmony with nature, mythological and heroic expression takes over the *récit*. Even the language seems to be self-alienating as words lose their everyday meaning, and Jean-Baptiste is lead into an imaginary world:

> Je jouissais de ma propre nature. . . . De
> la même manière j'ai toujours aimé renseigner
> les passants dans la rue, leur donner du feu,
> prêter la main aux charrettes trop lourdes.
> (*La Chute*, p. 1486)

Clearly this natural series leads to separations: Jean-Baptiste is carried even further into the heroism that alienates him:

> Parlons plutôt de ma courtoisie. Elle était
> célèbre et pourtant indiscutable. La politesse
> me donnait en effet de grandes joies. Si j'a-
> vais la chance, certains matins, de céder ma
> place, dans l'autobus ou le métro, à qui la
> méritait visiblement, de ramasser quelque ob-
> jet qu'une vieille avait laissé tomber . . .
> ou simplement de céder mon taxi à une personne
> plus pressée que moi, ma journée en était
> éclairée. . . . Quitter enfin mon fauteuil,
> au théâtre, pour permettre à un couple d'être
> réuni, placer en voyage les valises d'une jeune
> fille dans le filet placé trop haut pour elle,
> étaient autant d'exploits que j'accomplissais
> plus souvent que d'autres parce que j'étais
> plus attentif aux occasions de le faire et que
> j'en retirais des plaisirs mieux savourés.
> (*La Chute*, p. 1488)

In Jean-Baptiste's own words, he attained "la vie en prise directe" (p. 1489):

> Oui, peu d'êtres ont été plus naturels que moi.
> Mon accord avec la vie était total.
> *(La Chute,* p. 1489)

He maintained $\Delta = 0$ along with narcissism and the continuity of the *toujours déjà* factor: [J]e savais déjà tout en naissant. *(La Chute,* p. 489).

> Je passais aussi pour généreux et je l'étais. J'ai beaucoup donné en public et dans le privé. Mais loin de souffrir quand il fallait me séparer d'un objet ou d'une somme d'argent j'en tirais de constants plaisirs dont le moindre n'était pas une sorte de mélancolie qui, parfois, naissait en moi, à la considération de la stérilité de ces dons et de l'ingratitude probable qui les suivrait.
> *(La Chute,* p. 1487)

The traffic incident illustrates the natural order that orders movement with the light. The traumatic event happens because Jean-Baptiste does not move with the light; and he is a victim of the scene because he has not found the power to lead the game. But even in explicitly direct contrast to the "change without charge" of his present crossings in Amsterdam, his harmonious movement with the light, its ruptures, precision, and continuity form an unsatisfactory solution insofar as the mathematical exchange removes him consistently from life. The memory is as follows and portrays the same pattern we have seen before:

> Sans cesse, de nouvelles îles apparaissaient sur le cercle de l'horizon. Leur échine sans arbres traçait la limite du ciel, leur rivage rocheux tranchait nettement sur la mer. Aucune confusion; dans la lumière précise tout était repère. . . . J'avais l'impression de bondir. . . .
> *(La Chute,* p. 1525)

Jean-Baptiste had lost the exterior, and in his resulting narcissistic state, immobility and continuity condemned him:

> [J]'ai plané, littéralement, pendant des années dont, à vrai dire, j'ai encore le regret au cœur. J'ai plané jusqu'au soir où... Mais non, ceci est une autre affaire et il faut l'oublier. D'ailleurs, j'exagère peut-être. J'étais à l'aise en tout, il est vrai, mais en même temps satisfait de rien. Chaque joie m'en faisait désirer une autre. J'allais de fête en fête. Il m'arrivait de danser pendant des nuits, de plus en plus fou des êtres et de la vie.
>
> (*La Chute*, p. 1490)

The movement with light or altitude naturally leads to the denaturalization of the *je* and expressions of continuity. His freedom and the ability to exist depended upon his removal from the world, a phenomenon of which Jean-Baptiste is thoroughly aware:

> Arrêtons-nous sur ces cimes. Vous comprenez maintenant ce que je voulais dire en parlant de viser plus haut. Je parlais justement de ces points culminants, les seuls où je puisse vivre. Oui, je ne me suis jamais senti à l'aise que dans les situations élevées. Jusque dans le détail de la vie, j'avais besoin d'être au-dessus. Je préférais l'autobus au métro, les calèches aux taxis, les terrasses aux entresols. Amateur des avions de sport où l'on porte la tête en plein ciel, je figurais aussi, sur les bateaux, l'éternel promeneur des dunettes. En montagne, je fuyais les vallées encaissées pour les cols et les plateaux; j'étais l'homme des pénéplaines, au moins. Si le destin m'avait obligé de choisir un métier manuel, tourneur ou couvreur, soyez tranquille, j'eusse choisi les toits et fait amitié avec les vertiges. Les soutes, les cales, les souterrains, les grottes, les gouffres me faisaient horreur. J'avais même voué une haine spéciale aux spéléologues.
>
> (*La Chute*, p. 1489)

Jean-Baptiste even recognizes the fact that his continuity was based on the lack of the resemblance factor:

> Moi, moi, moi, voilà le refrain de ma chère vie, et qui s'entendait dans tout ce que je disais. Je n'ai jamais pu parler qu'en me vantant, surtout si je le faisais avec cette fracassante discrétion dont j'avais le secret. Il est bien vrai que j'ai toujours vécu libre et puissant. Simplement, je me sentais libéré à l'égard de tous pour l'excellente raison que je ne me reconnaissais pas d'égal. Je me suis toujours estimé plus intelligent que tout le monde, je vous l'ai dit, mais aussi plus sensible et plus adroit, tireur d'élite, conducteur incomparable, meilleur amant. Même dans les domaines où il m'était facile de vérifier mon infériorité.
> (*La Chute*, p. 1500)

> Quelle que fût, d'ailleurs, la confusion apparente de mes sentiments, le résultat que j'obtenais était clair: je maintenais toutes mes affections autour de moi pour m'en servir quand je le voulais.
> (*La Chute*, p. 1510)

Lead by the light, his *moi* was literally climbing, filled with itself, and associated with a language which evokes mathematics and ruptures. Even the final words of the passage cited below point to the absence of the *fond*, of which Valéry reminds us so very often: "assez pour avoir envie *d'aller au fond*." (*Cahiers*, p. 309):

> Quand je m'occupais d'autrui, c'était pure condescendance, en toute liberté, et le mérite entier m'en revenait: je montais d'un degré dans l'amour que je me portais.
> Avec quelques autres vérités, j'ai découvert ces évidences peu à peu, dans la période qui suivit le soir dont je vous ai parlé. Pas tout de suite, non, ni très distinctement. Il a fallu d'abord que je retrouve la mémoire. Par degrés, j'ai vu plus clair, j'ai appris un peu de ce que je savais. Jusque-là, j'avais toujours été aidé par un étonnant pouvoir

> d'oubli. J'oubliais tout, et d'abord mes réso-
> lutions. Au fond, rien ne comptait.
> (La Chute, p. 1500)

He realizes the fault of this first narcissism:

> Mais on ne peut souhaiter la mort de tout le
> monde ni, à la limite, dépeupler la planète
> pour jouir d'une liberté inimaginable autrement.
> (La Chute, p. 1510)

He had become the sun:

> Je ne pouvais donc vivre, de mon aveu même,
> qu'à la condition que, sur toute la terre, tous
> les êtres, ou le plus grand nombre possible,
> fussent tournés vers moi, éternellement vacants,
> privés de vie indépendante, prêts à répondre
> à mon appel à n'importe quel moment, voués en-
> fin à la stérilité, jusqu'au jour où je dai-
> gnerais les favoriser de ma lumière. En somme,
> pour que je vive heureux, il fallait que les
> êtres que j'élisais ne vécussent point.
> (La Chute, p. 1510)

In relationships with women, he expresses the same thing:

> [M]a partenaire à nouveau oubliée, je relui-
> sais. . . .
> (La Chute, p. 1509)

While his profession, in the name of justice, was based upon lies pretending to be truth, the following passage reveals again the lies, the light, the failure, the altitude, immobility, and the continuity. These elements form again a concise statement of the terms that lead Jean-Baptiste's life, and here the resemblance factor is still missing:

> Je me souviens encore avec tendresse de cer-
> taines nuits où j'allais dans une boîte sor-
> dide, retrouver une danseuse à transformations
> qui m'honorait de ses faveurs et pour la gloire
> de laquelle je me battis même, un soir, avec
> un barbillon vantard. Je paradais toutes les
> nuits au comptoir, dans la lumière rouge et la
> poussière de ce lieu de délices, mentant comme
> un arracheur de dents et buvant longuement.
> J'attendais l'aube, j'échouais enfin dans le

> lit toujours défait de ma princesse qui se li-
> vrait mécaniquement au plaisir, puis dormait
> sans transition. Le jour venait doucement
> éclairer ce désastre et je m'élevais, immobile,
> dans un matin de gloire.
> (*La Chute*, p. 1528)

Likewise, he was elected Pope:

> Mais j'ai bu l'eau. . . . [J]e devais me con-
> server à eux. C'est ainsi, cher, que naissent
> les empires et les églises, sous le soleil de
> la mort.
> (*La Chute*, p. 1541)

This sun of *death* is exactly what Jean-Baptiste had to remedy. Without the *other* or exterior, deferal becomes virtually impossible. In the realization of the complete narcissistic lie, Clamence seeks out an exterior that does not remove him from it, but one that provides him with an exchange that will be his power. This conversion is the result of the assimilation of difference as it occurs after the "brusque volte-face" over the bridge. In the account of the incident of laughter, Jean-Baptiste stresses the disappearing stars, the darkening sky, the glowing river, the street lamps, and the memory of summer:

> Voyez-vous, cher monsieur, c'était un beau soir
> d'automne, encore tiède sur la ville, déjà hu-
> mide sur la Seine. La nuit venait, le ciel
> était encore clair à l'ouest, mais s'assombris-
> sait, les lampadaires brillaient faiblement.
> Je remontais les quais de la rive gauche vers
> le pont des Arts. On voyait luire le fleuve,
> entre les boîtes fermées des bouquinistes.
> Il y avait peu de monde sur les quais: Paris
> mangeait déjà. Je foulais les feuilles jaunes
> et poussiéreuses qui rappelaient encore l'été.
> Le ciel se remplissait peu à peu d'étoiles
> qu'on apercevait fugitivement en s'éloignant
> d'un lampadaire vers un autre. Je goûtais le
> silence revenu, la douceur du soir. Paris vide.
> (*La Chute*, p. 1494)

All the above images emphasize the loss of direct light and
the birth of the glowing form--a form that does not open to
the natural succession but remains:

> On voit parfois plus clair dans celui qui ment
> que dans celui qui dit vrai. La vérité, comme
> la lumière, aveugle. Le mensonge, au contraire,
> est un beau crépuscule, qui met chaque objet
> en valeur.
> (*La Chute*, p. 1537)

The glowing form is suitably found in Amsterdam. As far as
natural light or fire is concerned, the present point of view
constantly reminds us of the ceaseless rain, as well as piles
of ashes and smoke, steaming water, and the cold--all elements
which extinguish the power of natural continuity. Instead,
the forms of Clamence's expression fill with pressure, marking
once again the movement without movement. The *genièvre*'s purpose is to put light within its subjects:

> Sentez-vous la lumière dorée, cuivrée qu'il
> met en vous?
> (*La Chute*, pp. 1481-1482)

The *cœurs* of the *récit débordent*, mouths fill with words, the
people of Amsterdam amass within a small space, and the contrast of hot and cold creates an inverse or dead world revived
only thorugh the speaker: the resulting duplicity is the mark
of his power:

> Mais c'est le trop-plein: dès que j'ouvre la
> bouche, les phrases coulent. Ce pays m'inspire
> d'ailleurs. J'aime ce peuple, grouillant sur
> les trottoirs, coincé dans un petit espace de
> maisons et d'eaux cerné par des brumes, des
> terres froides, et la mer fumante comme une
> lessive. Je l'aime car il est double. Il est
> ici et il est ailleurs.
> (*La Chute*, pp. 1481-1482)

The glowing light within images of pervading darkness, the insistance upon poetry, dreams, separations, circularity, and departures (or movements that really go nowhere)--all serve to sustain the existence of the self within the movement towards the *other*:

> Mais oui! A écouter leurs pas lourds, sur le pavé gras, à les voir passer pesamment entre leurs boutiques, pleines de harengs dorés et de bijoux couleur de feuilles mortes, vous croyez sans doute qu'ils sont là, ce soir? Vous êtes comme tout le monde, vous prenez ces braves gens pour une tribu de syndics et de marchands, comptant leurs écus avec leurs chances de vie éternelle, et dont le seul lyrisme consiste à prendre parfois, couverts de larges chapeaux, des leçons d'anatomie? Vous vous trompez. Ils marchent près de nous, il est vrai, et pourtant, voyez où se trouvent leurs têtes: dans cette brume de néon, de genièvre et de menthe qui descend des enseignes rouges et vertes. La Hollande est un songe, monsieur, un songe d'or et de fumée, plus fumeux le jour, plus doré la nuit, et nuit et jour ce songe est peuplé de Logengrin comme ceux-ci, filant rêveusement sur leurs noires bicyclettes à hauts guidons, cygnes funèbres qui tournent sans trêve, dans tout le pays, autour des mers, le long des canaux. Ils rêvent, la tête dans leurs nuées cuivrées, ils roulent en rond, ils prient, somnambules, dans l'encens doré de la brume, ils ne sont plus là. Ils sont partis à des milliers de kilomètres, vers Java, l'île lointaine. Ils prient ces dieux grimaçants de l'Indonésie dont ils ont garni toutes leurs vitrines, et qui errent en ce moment au-dessus de nous, avant de s'accrocher, comme des signes somptueux, aux enseignes et aux toits en escaliers, pour rappeler à ces colons nostalgiques que la Hollande n'est pas seulement l'Europe des marchands, mais la mer, la mer qui mène à Cipango, et à ces îles où les hommes meurent fous et heureux.
> (*La Chute*, p. 1482)

The lyrical digression takes over the *récit*, as Jean-Baptiste imagines far away and unattainable places whose destination (as the terminal point of a movement or departure) incorporates terms of death. Subsequent departures and confinement overtake the *récit*:

> Mais je me laisse aller, je plaide! Pardonnez-moi. L'habitude, monsieur, la vocation, le désir aussi où je suis de bien vous faire comprendre cette ville, et le cœur des choses! Car nous sommes au cœur des choses. Avez-vous remarqué que les canaux concentriques d'Amsterdam ressemblent aux cercles de l'enfer? L'enfer bourgeois, naturellement peuplé de mauvais rêves. Quand on arrive de l'extérieur, à mesure qu'on passe ces cercles, la vie, et donc ses crimes, devient plus épaisse, plus obscure. Ici, nous sommes dans le dernier cercle. Le cercle des... Ah! Vous savez cela? Diable, vous devenez plus difficile à classer. Mais vous comprenez alors pourquoi je puis dire que le centre des choses est ici, bien que nous nous trouvions à l'extrémité du continent. Un homme sensible comprend ces bizarreries. En tout cas, les lecteurs de journaux et les fornicateurs ne peuvent aller plus loin. Ils viennent de tous les coins de l'Europe et s'arrêtent autour de la mer intérieure, sur la grève décolorée. Ils écoutent les sirènes, cherchent en vain la silhouette des bateaux dans la brume, puis repassent les canaux et s'en retournent à travers la pluie. Transis, ils viennent demander, en toutes langues, du genièvre à *Mexico-City*. Là, je les attends.
> (*La Chute*, p. 1482-1483)

The coexistence of the extremity and the center, the darkness, rain, immobility, the wish to depart or for something to happen, the "vain," the various expressions of confinement and the call to the *other* side, direct the course of the *récit's* present path against natural or direct light and its effects. The people of Amsterdam cannot leave for the other shore, the gods descend, but the islands go off course, doves wish to descend, Clamence wants something to happen, etc. . . . And by the end of the *récit*, Clamence's fever is high and climbing:

> Je m'abandonne . . . à la fièvre qu'avec délices je sens monter en ce moment.
> (*La Chute*, p. 1548)

The blanket weighs on him, the heat rises, he is locked in his room, he is bedridden, and once again he is his own "forme fatale." Altitudes have progressively succeeded in overtaking his life once again:

> J'ai encore trouvé un sommet, où je . . . suis seul à grimper. . . .
> (*La Chute*, p. 1548)

> Alors je grandis, très cher, je grandis, je respire librement, je suis sur la montagne, la plaine s'étend sous mes yeux. Quelle ivresse de se sentir Dieu le père et de distribuer des certificats définitifs de mauvaise vie et mœurs. Je trône parmi mes vilains anges, à la cime du ciel hollandais, je regarde monter vers moi, sortant des brumes et de l'eau, la multitude du jugement dernier. Ils s'élèvent lentement, je vois arriver déjà le premier d'entre eux. Sur sa face égarée, à moitié cachée par une main, je lis la tristesse de la condition commune, et le désespoir de ne pouvoir y échapper. Et moi, je plains sans absoudre, je comprends sans pardonner et surtout, ah, je sens enfin que l'on m'adore!
> Oui, je m'agite, comment resterais-je sagement couché?
> (*La Chute*, p. 1549)

The miracles and paradox of his speech depict an explosion, and they have paradoxically taken the narcissistic lie one step too far: the link has been taken out of difference in spite of the final effort to confer reflections upon the *other* in the assimilation of her. The final words of the *récit* succeed in maintaining ambiguity:

> Il sera toujours trop tard.
> (*La Chute*, p. 1551)

Once and for all, continuity and immobility resemble one another: we can never really know whether Clamence has become *other* or simply remained immobile. The narcissistic lie has succeeded in confusing natural order.

II.

Literal Distortions, the Hypothesis, and Foreshadows of the Coincidence

Examining the possibility of one text rewriting another, the hypothesis tests the relationship between Camus's *récit*, *La Chute*, and Dante's *Commedia*. Let us consider the latter in terms of a dynamic force, capable of engendering to some large degree Camus's last work: I will refer to the latter as the rewriting.

The form of intertextuality with which the hypothesis concerns itself anticipates *La Chute*'s literal level through the associations provided by the *Commedia* but without claiming that such reader-recognition is necessary for a clear understanding of the language of Camus's *juge-pénitent*. If one chooses to recognize Clamence's language as intertextual, the resulting rewriting gradually confirms its own validity in the form of isotopes: the appearance of interwoven narrative threads, contrary to the *récit*'s own account, proves that intertextuality can give way to the formation of isotopes. (I therefore use neither Greimas' nor Adam's definitions of the term.) Occasional explicit allusions to Dante's *Inferno* are only a further confirmation of the gradual surfacing of the Dantesque presence to the literal level and become metacritical:

    Connaissez-vous Dante?
                        (p. 1518)

Such explicit commentary is not our principal concern, since it is only after the fact proof of the gradually emerging motivational force. I will examine the possible concretion of isotopes with respect to density, repetition, and specificity.

Through the associations permitted by the *Commedia*, the reader anticipates *La Chute*'s language, images, questions raised regarding literal and figurative meaning, the limits of language, and problems in interpretation. Perhaps most convincing and most present in *La Chute* as a rewriting are its Dantesque characters. Even if all these elements are somewhat present in *La Chute*'s own coherent structure (after all, they are part of the text's literal level), the weight of the words given by the double perspective is not. The new dimension acquired through the rewriting is most precisely literary, insofar as the words themselves become the principal focus of our attention. Without underscoring the meaningfulness of form as pretext (for psychological, historical, political, sociological, thermodynamic, biological, tropic, archetypal, and other structural models), the new perspective of the text's *littérarité* is an important mark of its fully realized existence--fully realized with respect to its "multiplicity of possible translations"[1] as well as its *poetic* sense.

To allow the *Commedia* to rewrite *La Chute* one expects irony, parody, and other terms of reversals and negations to result. A few examples from the first part of Clamence's *récit* (p. 1477) illustrate this: "L'estimable gorille qui préside aux destinées de cet établissement," "notre taciturne ami" who disdains the civilized languages, the job of the barman which "consiste

à recevoir des marins de toutes les nationalités dans ce bar
d'Amsterdam qu'il a appelé d'ailleurs, on ne sait pourquoi,
Mexico-City," or the "Cro-Magnon" gorilla-barman described as
a "pensionnaire à la tour de Babel."

These expressions contain an obvious undercutting element
without the presence of the *Commedia*: they either contain a
contradiction and/or an element out of place; but if one adds
to these factors that the barman is actually Ulysses, that the
civilized languages are substituted for the vulgar ones, that
the mythological lake of Cocytus has been turned into a bar,
Nimrod into a Cro-Magnon, and ultimately an ascent into a fall,
the undercutting becomes all the more powerful. Even if reversals, lies, parody, irony, and other forms of negation are
inherent to *La Chute* and to other modes of textual analysis as
presented in Genette's various aspects of *transtextualité* or in
Bloom's *Map of Misreading*,[2] they do not lose their significance
as elements of the rewriting process. On the contrary, the
Commedia shows itself to be all the better "chosen" for the rewriting, and the rewritten *récit* to be all the more realized
as a literary work (if one permits such terms as those which
come forth again and again in so many methods of approaching
literature to be the mark of validity).

While *La Chute* and the *Commedia* are so far removed from one
another in so many ways, their outward similarities as well
as their direct oppositions make their unity more plausible.
While the voice of *La Chute*, independently of the *Commedia*, is
conscious of its digressions, its "envolées professionnelles"

(p. 1509), the "flights" of language and splits between meaning and words take place in the progress of the *récit* as well as in the progress of Clamence-pilgrim; the presence of Dante's "sacred poem" outlines so clearly the *récit*'s path towards decapitation, miracles, paradox, inversions, and the final plunge. Contrary to the *Commedia*'s path, the *récit* immobilizes itself progressively through its words--an immobilization of which its characteristic aphorisms are a mark as well as Clamence's constant fascination with his own words:

> [J]e ne pouvais rencontrer un homme d'esprit sans qu'aussitôt j'en fisse ma société. . . .
> [V]ous bronchez sur cet imparfait du subjonctif. J'avoue ma faiblesse pour ce mode. . . .
> (p. 1548)

The process occurs repeatedly. If not the use of a word, it is often his lyricism as, for example, when he actually has to interrupt one of his poetic flights of language:

> Arretêz-moi! Je deviens lyrique.
> (p. 1525)

More interesting than these exterior signs is the actual fascination with literal meaning and its ability to deform and contaminate the *récit*, a phenomenon of which one of the best examples (already discussed somewhat in Chapter One) is found in Jean-Baptiste's following words:

> [J]'admettais les sauterelles.
> (p. 1484)

Of course, locusts are logically to be expected where John the Baptist is of concern, and Jean-Baptiste's namesake has been shown to be present throughout the *récit* on an explicitly recognizable level. But Jean-Baptiste goes so far as to let the literal meaning of his words engender his discourse as he drifts into the subject of locusts:

> [L]es invasions de ces orthoptères ne m'ont jamais rapporté un centime. . . .
> (p. 1485)

While the religious parody is an obvious result of the literal extension, more important is the power of literal meaning to create an inverted world, parallel to the inversion created by the *contrapasso* of Dante's *Inferno*. Also, Jean-Baptiste's very unusual choice of words often marks his discourse. For example, his reference to the "forêts primitives" (p. 1477) is not a usual combination of words in the French language. Similarly, stressed usage of relatively odd vocabulary, as seen in the high frequency of the *enseignes*, draws the reader to dwell upon the literal level. But most importantly active in this literal deformation, are any of the realized isotopes of the rewriting: narrative threads of elements identifying the Dantesque presence stress the literal level and disfigure the figurative to make use of literal meaning.

One must recall that even though words in the *Commedia*, are the means to reaching that point where words no longer mask reality, the pilgrim's desire must take him beyond them. He must literally turn from his former poetry (his *Rime Petrose*) during his descent into the *Inferno*'s lower depths so as to avoid petrification. Before entering Dis, he must literally turn from the Medusa to avoid turning to stone or the immobility which is a mark of all the *Inferno*, culminating in the last circle of Cocytus--the frozen lake at the physical center of the Earth, realm of Compound Fraud or Treachery, the most "immobilizing" of sins through its perversion of bonds. Massive towers, actually giants like Nimrod, are its guardians and the guardians of Lucifer who finds himself immobilized in the ice of the lake's center. Cocytus also includes the Treacherous Hosts. It is also the setting for a horrible parody of the Word made Flesh: Ugolino's tale, the most tragic of the *Inferno*, leads one to take him literally in his cannibalism and therefore to understand his ambiguous words in the worst possible sense when he says:

'Poscia, più che il dolor, potè 'l digiuno.'[3]
(*Inferno* XXXIII, 75)

Through the emphasis on chewing, the mouth, bread, hunger, the children's offers of their own flesh to their starving father,[4] and the religiously significant numerical references regarding the children's deaths in the passage from the fifth to sixth day[5]--all elements point to the interpretation that a parody of the Eucharist is in the making: the result is Ugolino's cannibalism.

All the way through the *Inferno* words call attention to themselves as a medium; on the Gates of Hell in the massive lettering of the inscription, in Nimrod's garbled speech, and in the power of literature and words to divert the reader: illustrations of this are found in the *canti* of Paolo and Francesca who died as a result of their misuse of literature, Ser Brunetto who taught men "how to make themselves eternal" through literature, and Ulysses who persuaded his men to go off the straight path. Likewise, words serve to mask the sin through the tragic and heroic renderings for which Ulysses and Ugolino are famed. The emphasis on language culminates in the power of the literal meaning of words to create an inverted reality, of which Dante's *Inferno* is the impure mark in its use of "dead poetry," and most visibly inverted in its use of the *contrapasso*; for example, Ulysses in the "tongue of fire,"[6] Paolo and Francesca caught in the "whirlwind of passion,"[7] or the hypocrites who are literally "gilded over."[8] The *Inferno* is marked as a permanent and visible realm, the most traditionally comprehensible for the reader, and the canticle where the sinners remain eternally bound and blind to their sin, unlike the souls of the transitory state of the *Purgatorio*, where every soul is a traveller, and unlike the *Paradiso*, characterized by its souls who have only "condescended" to appear. The third canticle is characterized by paradox[9] and reflections,[10] and Beatrice has explained to the pilgrim that here the reflection is the only reality: impurities are necessary for the mortal visitor's comprehension. The language of the *Paradiso* tends to its own effacement, while the *Inferno* is a permanent impurity and the *Purgatorio* a temporal state.

The inversions, reflections, and paradox of the *Commedia* appear very suited to the *récit* which claims duplicity, inversion, and revelation as its goals. While the *Commedia* tells of an ascent and *La Chute* of a fall, they share the common usage of flight imagery and the sea-going voyage, exile and bondage and freedom, three important moments of dove imagery, judgement of contemporaries and of history, confession, self-purgation, conversion, reflections (in the mirror's sense), the division or forgetfulness of self,[11] islands, canals, dikes, bridges, boats, crossings, a guide, rain, cold, references to the right and left, circular and linear motion, fog, memory, rivers, the call of a female figure, dreams, the final plunge, the central theme of love,[12] John the Baptist, the last circle, and the question of a silent accomplice (parallel to Ulysses' silent accomplice to the theft of the Palladium) as portrayed in Clamence's silent listener, invited to share in human guilt. To all of the above, one should add all those isotopes which reveal themselves to be a part of the rewriting process. The use of dramatic monologue and literary and imperfect tenses, along with the insistance on memory, also suggests the sinners of the *Inferno* who speak at length on their past lives while masking and refusing the error; the tone of Camus-Clamence's *récit* parallels the tone of those souls so often obsessed by being remembered on Earth. In part six of his monologue, Camus's character takes the final plunge--if we allow ourselves to take him literally. As for the *Commedia*, at the end of the pilgrim's flight and at that moment of the beatific vision:

> A l'alta fantasia qui mancò possa.
> (*Paradiso* XXXIII, 142)

His perspective falls below the surface of the ocean, as it is expressed in terms of Neptune seeing the shadow of the Argo pass over him:

>   Un punto solo m'è maggior letargo
>   Che venticinque secoli a la impresa
>   Che fè Nettuno ammirar l'ombra d'Argo.
>   (*Paradiso*, XXXIII, 94-96)

The perspective is ironically that of a failure, but the presumption is still there as Dante pilgrim compares himself to a new Jason. While Dante's text tends towards unity--the unity of that point where words no longer mask reality as they do in the *Inferno*, Camus's text tends towards separation and duplicity.

Perhaps many of the above elements tend to appear archetypal, or biblical, but the rewriting will show them to be caught up in a form of isotope, one in which, instead of only revealing a previously established series of events, includes details outside the events of the narration--as in whether or not to take the character's words literally.

After the fact elements which show the relationship to be not so farfetched include the roles of Saint Augustine, the city of Florence, and Ulysses. As for Saint Augustine, even if Camus's knowledge of him is claimed to be superficial,[13] he wrote a thesis dealing with the relationship between Hellenism and Christianity through Plotinus and Augustine,[14] and Augustine played an important role in Camus's life.[15] In regard to Florence, Dante's birthplace and the city from which he was exiled, Camus writes:

>   Rimbaud finit en Abyssinie sans avoir écrit une
>   seule ligne. . . . Je saisissais le balance-
>   ment qui mène certains hommes de l'ascèse à
>   la jouissance et du dépouillement à la profes-
>   sion dans la volupté. J'admirais, j'admire
>   ce lien qui, au monde, unit l'homme, ce double

> reflet dans lequel mon cœur peut intervenir
> et dicter son bonheur jusqu'à une limite précise
> où le monde peut alors l'achever ou le détruire.
> Florence! Un des seuls lieux d'Europe où j'ai
> compris qu'au cœur de ma révolte dormait un
> consentement.[16]

Florence is seen therefore as a destiny, and one should not hesitate to include John the Baptist within this presence, since he is the patron saint of Dante's birthplace and remains present throughout the *Commedia*, and since Camus's *juge-pénitent* bears his name. In regard to John the Baptist's presence within *La Chute*--that is, as an underlying force behind some of the subject matter and language of Jean-Baptiste's *récit*, Adèle King and Jacqueline Lévi-Valensi have studied it to some degree.[17]

In regard to Ulysses, Camus writes:

> L'année de la guerre je devais m'embarquer pour
> refaire le périple d'Ulysse.[18]

While Camus often alludes to Ulysses in his essays, one must recall that Dante's Ulysses is far from Homer's, since he constructed the character as undertaking an anti-voyage, one against which the path of the *Commedia* takes shape, all the while taking literal and thematic echoes from it to reach a point which corrects and goes beyond it. The process is used throughout the *Commedia*, and ultimately offers the correction of the "error" or wandering from the straight path. Since Ulysses is constructed as an anti-hero, his episode is obviously the most extensive concerning the technique, or as Lansing words it:

> The Ulysses episode and various passages
> throughout the poem which are related to it
> thematically constitute a fundamental pattern
> of meaning in the *Commedia*. The noble Greek hero
> captures Dante's poetic imagination because
> the poet saw in this figure a vehicle for ex-
> pressing allegorically the *crise de conscience* that
> brought him to compose the great poem which
> is the *Commedia*. . . . From a detailed study .
> . . emerges sufficient evidence to determine
> the nature of the personal crisis which Dante
> allegorizes in the Prologue as a departure from
> the straight way and a temporary disappearance
> into the dark wood, and which motivates the
> journey to the other world and consequently
> the composition of the poem.[19]

Chiampi's discussion of the Francesca da Rimini episode of Canto V of the *Inferno* stresses the same process:

> The episode's presence is continually evoked
> in metrical echoes, . . . its key words re-
> peated until they become thematic nodes and
> its simple plot abstracted, recapitulated and
> ultimately even redeemed as the *littera*, the al-
> legorical surface, of an edifying message.[20]

Nowhere is it made evident that Camus was familiar with Dante's poem even though one can assume he was. While the Greek hero also has appealed to his poetic imagination, it is surprisingly enough Dante's Ulysses who comes forth in *La Chute*. Of course, the specificity never reveals exact correspondences between Dante's and Camus's characters, situations, and corresponding language, nor a logical ordering in the diegesis of textual elements--that is, a clear reversal of the elements as they appear in the *Commedia*. As for Dante's elements, they may very well contaminate or rewrite more than one of *La Chute*'s: for example, Dante's Ulysses contaminates many characters, situations, and much of the language and thought of the *récit*. Dispersion is the rule, particularly since authorial intent is of no concern.

The rewriting process reveals itself through selected passages of *La Chute* which contain the intertextual seeds of their Dantesque roots. In a step-by-step reading, I will establish the context of these elements within the *Commedia* while emphasizing the most immediate associations. The next logical step is to continue reading with the expectation that enough anticipated elements surface to the literal level--through density, repetition, and specificity--for one to conclude that a rewriting is at work. If intertextuality really can lead to the formation of isotopes, the rewriting process proves a valid means of reading, and *La Chute* discovers a new literary dimension.

Footnotes to Chapter II

¹ "[T]he fecundity of a producer of ideas is proven by the multiplicity of possible translations (interpretations)" (Albert Camus's 1949 Notebook [Monnerot], p. 222, quoted in and translated by Donald Lazère, *The Unique Creation of Albert Camus* [New Haven: Yale University Press, 1973], p. 24).

² Harold Bloom, *A Map of Misreading* (New York: Oxford University Press, 1975).

³ All references to and citations from the *Commedia* follow the text established by C. H. Grandgent, ed., *"La divina commedia" di Dante Alighieri* (Boston: D. C. Heath & Co., 1933).

⁴ *Inferno* XXXIII, 1-3, 23, 36, 39, 59, 62-63, 75, 77.

⁵ "Quivi morì; e come tu me vedi,/Vid' io cascar li tre ad uno ad une/Tra 'l quinto dì e 'l sesto. . . ." (Ibid., 71-72).

⁶ "Quand les jours de la Pentecôte furent accomplis les disciples étant tous ensemble dans un même lieu, on entendit tout d'un coup un grand bruit, comme d'un vent impétueux, qui venait du ciel, . . ." (*Actes des Apôtres*, II, 1-11 quoted in Andre Pézard, *Dante sous la pluie de feu* [Paris: Vrin, 1950], p. 283); ". . . [I]ls virent paraître comme des langues de feu, qui se partagèrent et s'arrêtèrent sur chacun d'eux" (Ibid., p. 283); "Aux chants XXVI et XXVII voici paraitre les conseillers perfides, enfermés chacun dans une flamme qui marche et qui parle, et qui fait à chaque syllabe palpiter sa langue dorée. L'image est claire, mais elle s'explique mieux encore si on la rapproche de l'allégorie du chant XV châtiant les 'violences contre l'esprit'. Conseil, en effet, parmi les sept dons du saint Esprit, est l'un de ceux que Dante vénère par profession" (Pézard, *Dante sous la pluie de feu*, p. 287).

⁷ "In life, St. Augustine had glimpsed in his lust the punishment of the damned: 'I was tossed and spilled, floundering in the broiling sea of my fornication and you said no word...I deserted you and allowed myself to be carried away by the sweep of the tide'" (St. Augustine, *Confessions*, Book II, 2, quoted in James Thomas Chiampi, *Shadowy Prefaces: Conversion and Writing in the "Divine Comedy"* [Ravenna: Longo Editore, 1981], p. 69); Chiampi also points out the parallel structure in the syntax of the words used to describe the motion of the *contrapasso*: "Di qua, di là, di giù, di su li mena ['la bufera infernal']" (*Inferno* V, 43).

⁸ "The exact form of their punishment was probably suggested to Dante by the *Magnœ Derivationes* of Ugoccione da Pisa, who defines 'ypocrita' as 'superauratus,' . . ." (C. H.

Grandgent, ed. and annotated, *"La divina commedia" di Dante Alighieri*
[Boston: D. C. Heath & Co., 1933], p. 204).

[9] For example: "'Vergine Madre, figlia del tuo Figlio'"
(*Paradiso* XXXIII, 1); "Qual è 'l geometra che tutto s'affige/Per
misurar lo cerchio, e non ritrova/Pensando quel principio ond'
e li indige,/Tal era io a quella vista nova" (Ibid., 133-136);
Fontanier defines *le paradoxisme* in *Figures du discours* as consisting of two terms which seem to contradict one another but actually express a truer approximation of reality.

[10] For example: Nella profonda e chiara sussistenza/Dell'
alto lume parvermi tre giri/Di tre colori e d' una contenenza;/
E l' un dall' altro come iri da iri/Parea reflesso. . . ."
(*Paradiso* XXXIII, 116-120); "Tre specchi prenderai. . . . /Rivolto ad essi, fa che dopo il dosso/Ti stea un lume che i tre
specchi accenda/E torni a te da tutti ripercosso" (*Paradiso* II,
97-102);

> "Quali per vetri trasparenti e tersi,
>   O ver per acque nitide e tranquille,
>   Non sì profonde che i fondi sien persi,
> Tornan di nostri visi le postille
>   Debili sì, che prela in bianca fronte
>   Non vien men tosto alle nostre pupille;
> . . . .
> Subito sì com' io di lor m' accorsi,
>   Quelle stimando specchiati sembianti,
>   Per veder di cui fosser, li occhi torsi"
>   (*Paradiso* III, 10-21)

[11] Division from self or forgetfulness of self as a form
of error in the Augustinian sense of *obblio* is a constituent
element of both works.

[12] "Indeed love, just as in Dante's *Paradiso*, now becomes
the central theme of Baptiste's exposition" (Alfred Cordes,
The Descent of the Doves: Camus's Journey to the Spirit [Washington,
D. C.: University Press of America, 1980], p. 154).

[13] "Camus did not go deeply into Augustine and he relied
heavily on other people's interpretations" (Patrick McCarthy,
Camus [New York: Random House, 1982], p. 71).

[14] For a discussion of his *Thèse du troisième cycle*, see
Ibid., pp. 72-73.

[15] "Augustine became a hero of Algerian culture and, although not much read, he could be trotted out in the most implausible circumstances" (Ibid., p. 64).

[16] Camus, "Le Désert," in *Noces; L'Eté* (Paris: Gallimard,
Livre de Poche, 1959), p. 72.

[17] Jacqueline Lévi-Valensi, "*La Chute* ou la parole en procès," *La Revue des lettres modernes*, Nos. 238-244 (1970), p. 43.

[18] Camus, "Prométhée aux enfers," in *L'Eté*, in *Essais* (Paris: Gallimard, Bibliothèque de la Pléiade), p. 842; Camus actually made the trip (Roger Quillot, ed. and annotated, *Albert Camus: Théâtres, récits, nouvelles* [Paris: Gallimard, Bibliothèque de la Pléiade, 1962], p. 2055).

[19] Richard H. Lansing, "Patterns of Meaning: The Shipwrecked Swimmer and Elijah's Ascent," in *From Image to Idea: A Study of the Simile in Dante's "Commedia"* (Ravenna: Longo Editore, 1976), p. 94.

[20] James Thomas Chiampi, "Francesca da Rimini: From the Intransitive Moment to the Point," in *Shadowy Prefaces: Conversion and Writing in the "Divine Comedy"* (Ravenna: Longo Editore, 1981), p. 51.

III.

"Rewriting" the First Part of Clamence's Account: Suggestions and Concretions

One of the initially stressed elements of Camus's *récit* is the barman-host's animal nature:

> L'estimable gorille . . . préside aux destinées de cet établissement.
> (p. 1477)

The characteristic recurs:

> [C]'est le privilège des grands animaux.
> (p. 1477)

With the animal who presides over the world the reader is about to enter, one should anticipate having fallen into Dante's "selva oscura" of Canto I of the *Inferno*, the wood where the pilgrim's voyage begins. Camus's text soon provides a comparison between the barman's silence and the silence of forests:

> C'est le silence des forêts primitives. . . .
> (p. 1477)

The reader's suspicion is therefore confirmed in the deformation of such language to provide a literal image. Other elements which may confirm the rewriting are the use of "obscure" (p. 1483) and "obscurément" (p. 1478) and the barman-gorilla's "gravité ombrageuse" (p. 1478); such elements as these will not be the last of such occurrences, clearly lending themselves to a disfigurement which supports the rewriting. Another example occurs as follows:

> Mais la terre est obscure, cher ami, le bois épais. . . .
> (p. 1513)

Dante's "dark wood" has therefore gradually become a more concrete presence. On the subject of Dante's first canto, one should note Clamence's description of himself at the time just before which he "converted" or changed his direction in life:

> Mais imaginez . . . un homme dans la force de l'âge. . . .
> (p. 1489)

Furthermore, in Camus's previous works, Rieux of *La Peste* and Jonas of "Jonas ou l'artiste au travail" are both 35 years old. One is lead to imagine the possible underlying presence of Dante's pilgrim:

> Nel mezzo del cammin de nostra vita
> Mi ritrovai per una selva oscura,
> Che la diritta via era smarrita.
> (*Inferno* I, 1-3)

The disfigurement of *La Chute* proves all the more valid, as the *récit* situates itself predominantly in the *Inferno* and even goes so far as to announce the presence of "concentric circles," the "last circle," "Dante," the "Neutral Angels," the "vestibule," and other indices precisely or close to the metacritical. The *Inferno*, as the canticle of masking language, immobility, and the *contrapasso* (in which the literal meaning gives way to reality) is an inverted world culminating in the frozen lake of Cocytus, the last circle, where the ultimate immobilization and parody of the Word take place. In *La Chute*, as Clamence tries to place his *récit* as lying on the road to his own version of the beatific vision, he increasingly pigeonholes himself into this inverted and dead world, the canticle of "dead poetry."[1]

It may seem a contradiction to speak of the overwhelming presence of the last circle of the *Inferno* when the initial passage of the *récit* strongly suggests the underlying presence of the arrival in the "dark wood;" but I prefer to hypothesize that all suggested elements of the *Commedia* are drawn towards the last circle. Such a process would depict a fall from all points of view, since Dante's pilgrim "converts" at the last circle: what was down is now up, therefore to return to the last circle is always a fall indicating a gravitational force of which Jean-Baptiste finds himself the origin or central point of earth. The hypothesized fall is not alone in producing the multiplicity conferred upon the *récit* by the rewriting. Multiplicity results from other factors as well.

Let us now return to the "dark wood" of Camus's "forêts primitives" in a metaphorical expression of the host's silence. The animal nature is clearly a dominant trait of the barman-gorilla's nature and suggests Dante's three beasts who prevent the pilgrim's direct ascent to the light of the mountain, thematically and verbally echoed in the island of Purgatory. Wild animal traits succeed in contaminating Clamence's Dutch inhabitants at numerous instances and eventually Clamence himself. From the gorilla, to the "fort bourgeoises créatures" (p. 1479), to an obsession with creatures, primates, snakes, "fauves" (p. 1515), and to the recurrent *forêts*, the *récit* arrives at that point where Clamence says, "Comme si mon véritable désir n'était pas d'être la créature . . ." (pp. 1503-1504). The assimilation proves an important mark of the rewriting as well as of the *récit* itself. As a rule, the isotopes of the rewriting always converge upon Clamence: he realizes them, assimilates them to the first person of the *récit* with complete disregard for time, place, and his own intent, as if a centrifugal force were constantly at work with Jean-Baptiste at the center--the center of the last circle, of all precipitation, and of all immobilization. (Camus's preoccupation with turning to stone is an overwhelming presence of his previous works, and most often it appears in conjunction with elements which could again evoke the *Inferno*. Regarding immobilization, the role of the prison cell is also so prevalent in Camus's previous works and certainly suited to the recurrent obsession with judgement.) Such is the destiny of the pilgrim having arrived onto the shore foreseen in the "forêts primitives" of the *récit*'s opening passage. Besides, the *Commedia* begins in the "dark wood" when the pilgrim implicitely awakens from Ulysses' shipwreck to begin the corrective journey:

> E come quei che, con lena affanata,
> Uscito fuor del pelago a la riva,
> Si volge a l'acqua perigliosa e guata,
> Così l'animo mio, ch' ancor fuggiva,
> Si volse a rietro a rimirar lo passo
> Che non lasciò già mai persona viva.
> Poi ch' ei posato un poco il corpo lasso,
> Ripresi via per la piaggia diserta,
> Sì che 'l piè fermo sempre era 'l più basso.
>   (*Inferno* I, 22-30)

The literal element of the "desert shore" is present in both Canto I of the *Inferno* and Canto I of the *Purgatorio*. Both shores are points of conversion, at the base of mountains or islands, and Dante creates his Ulysses to meet his death upon the shore of an island, as he is deprived of divine light in his heroic pursuit of "virtue and knowledge." Dante-pilgrim however survives the shipwreck to arrive upon the shore. As three beasts prevent his direct passage, he must first descend (go through Hell in an undoing process of the self) before beginning the rebuilding of the *Purgatorio*. Jean-Baptiste also refuses an upward path:

> Je refusais cette pente de nature qui me porte irrésistiblement à la sympathie.
> (p. 1481)

Once again, the deformation of figurative language seems appropriate to Jean-Baptiste, and one is lead to take him literally. Jean-Baptiste does not reject Purgatory by any means; he simply does not accept an order which distinguishes it from Hell or from Paradise. Such a process condemns all elements to the lowest realm, since the internal trait is irreversibly contaminating. Furthermore, even in the *Commedia*, the *Inferno* is physically located in the Earth with Lucifer at its center in the last circle. Jean-Baptiste soon announces that he lives in a damned place when he specifies:

> [J]'habite sur les lieux d'un des plus grands crimes de l'histoire.
> (p. 1481)

Even though Clamence's explanation provides its own coherent definition for this "great crime," our anticipation of the "last circle" proves correct. The pervading elements of treachery, cold, and the identification of Amsterdam are dominant in Dante's last circle as well as in *La Chute*.

Let us return once again to the beginning of the *récit* to anticipate Nimrod's presence. In the *Inferno*, he is known as the designer of the tower of Babel, responsible for the differentiation, confusion, and decay of languages, and is condemned to babble unintelligible speech (*Inferno* XXXI, 67) and to blow a horn in a heroic parady of Roland (*Inferno* XXXI, 16-18). To Dante-pilgrim, he looks like a tower but is actually a giant (*Inferno* XXX, 20) and guardian of the central pit in which he is lodged. Ignorance, massiveness, the babble, and the heroic parody condemn his sin of pride. Scorn is also a dominant element of the episode, as Virgil makes his attitude towards the sinner known.

Dante compares his giants to Frieslanders (*Inferno* XXXI, 64). Along with canals, dikes, bridges, and water resembling a windmill (*Inferno* XXXII, 6) as he flaps his arms at the center of the lake, the *Inferno*'s indices suggest Holland, the setting for Clamence's tale.

It is immediately at the beginning of his *récit* that Jean-Baptiste speaks of the confusion of languages in his expression of "toutes les langues" (p. 1477), spoken at the famed bar of Mexico-City. Similarly, the literal function of "*Mexico-City*" within "Amsterdam" evokes the same confusion, particularly as Jean-Baptiste dwells upon "not knowing why" it has such a name. The scorn towards the barman is made all too obvious in the constant undercutting remarks:

> Je crains que vous ne sachiez vous faire entendre de l'estimable gorille qui préside aux destinées de cet établissement.
> (p. 1477)
>
> Voilà, j'ose espérer qu'il m'a compris; ce hochement de tête doit signifier qu'il se rend à mes arguments.
> (p. 1477)
>
> Etre roi de ses humeurs, c'est le privilège des grands animaux.
> (p. 1477)

The suspicious and scornful tone and ironic distance of the *récit* continue throughout but are particularly dense here in regard to the barman. Scorn happens to be an element which Dante's pilgrim learns to feel with more and more conviction as he progressively confronts the various categories of sinners. For Nimrod it is particularly strong, as he and Virgil make a point of walking right past the giant. In a similar manner, the "sage lenteur" (p. 1477) of Camus's barman hints at the giant's massive bulk. Also, the "silence assourdissant" (p. 1477) is described as "chargé jusqu'à la gueule," possibly suggesting the heroic sounding of the horn which Nimrod is condemned to blow as well as babble. These elements strengthen the identification and appear with greater density in the second paragraph of the *récit* than in the first. Even without the rewriting, it is evident that the *récit* sets out to assimilate incomprehensible and alienating speech. Similarly, the heroic and parodic tone is present within the text's own coherence. However, the text as a rewriting actually anticipates the literal level and provides unifying structures. One might even include the presence of excessive honking in Clamence's *récit* to consider the extensive episode in the illustration of isotopic formation: one must consider the possibility of a valid rewriting with the subsequent use of *gestes* along with "horns" at three instances and the increasingly heroic tone:

> Je faisais des gestes. . . . [N]os patients concitoyens déchaînaient sans délai leurs avertisseurs. . . . [Q]uelques avertisseurs commençaient, derrière moi, de se faire entendre. . . . [U]n concert d'avertisseurs s'éleva. . . . Je m'étais laissé battre sans répondre, mais on ne pouvait pas m'accuser de lâcheté. . . . [J]e brûlais de prendre ma revanche. . . .
> (pp. 1501-1503)

The traffic incident obviously has its place in the story of the *récit*, but is distorted in length and out of place; and while that which is out of place has a recurrent role within the text's own coherence, it is possible that the unifying structures provided by the rewriting play a valid role.

Nimrod's presence first appears in the initial lines of the *récit* with the barman who "préside aux destinées," suggesting the guardian; his job "consiste à recevoir des marins de toutes les nationalités dans ce bar d'Amsterdam qu'il a appelé d'ailleurs, on ne sait pourquoi, *Mexico-City*:" these elements are soon to recur in the people of Holland, who return from the "desert shore" (p. 1483) and ask "in all languages" (p. 1483) for some *genièvre* at Mexico-City (p. 1483). The juxtaposition of Mexico-City to the confusion of languages and the guardian presently suggests the identification of Nimrod. Soon after such suggestions in the first paragraph of the *récit*.

Clamence compares the barman to a Cro-Magnon, and the "tower" comes into play to provide "la tour de Babel:"

> Imaginez l'homme de Cro-Magnon pensionnaire
> à la tour de Babel!
> (p. 1477)

Exile and lack of speech subsequently become explicit subject matter of the *récit*:

> Mais non, celui-ci ne sent pas son exil, il va son chemin, rien ne l'entame. Une des rares phrases que j'aie entendues de sa bouche proclamait que c'était à prendre ou à laisser.
> (p. 1477)

The matter of massive bulk then becomes precise as Clamence describes his host as "tout d'une pièce," followed once again by references to the barman's defiant, ridiculous, and speechless nature:

> A force de ne pas comprendre ce qu'on dit en sa présence, il a pris un caractère défiant.
> (p. 1478)

A multitude of elements of Dante's first canticle present themselves in these initial lines, and "*Mexico-City*" could prove itself to be an imperfect anagram for *Cocyte*, particularly as it occurs both times (in the first portion of the *récit*) in conjunction with the diversity of languages. In the second and more conclusive instance of this, the diversity of languages occurs at that moment when Jean-Baptiste situates his account as taking place in the "last circle" (p. 1483); therefore, just as Nimrod is one of the guardians of Cocytus or of Lucifer, the gorilla-barman is one of the guardians of Jean-Baptiste's text, destined for the last circle and all its infernal implications.

Up until this point, a similar beginning point, the "dark wood," has been established for the journey of Clamence's fall and Dante-pilgrim's ascent. The resulting confusion between the first and last circles, with respect to the latter, is logical in the sense that survival of the shipwreck means either passage to Canto I of the *Inferno* or to Canto I of the *Purgatorio*, since both are shores of arrival, thematic continuity with respect to Ulysses' voyage.

Dante's Ulysses is the very first, the clearest, and one of the most productive elements of Camus's work viewed in terms of the rewriting. Proving to be the most major of such elements, it forms an important and all encompassing parallel with the *Commedia*, where the voyage of Ulysses serves as an anti-voyage for the entire poem.

For Clamence, it is first of all a question of understanding someone and needing an interpreter:

> Puis-je monsieur, vous proposer mes services sans risquer d'être importun? Je crains que vous ne sachiez vous faire entendre de l'estimable gorille qui préside aux destinées de cet établissement.
> (p. 1477)

These very first words of the *récit* recall precisely the situation at the beginning of Canto XXVI of the *Inferno*: Virgil decides he must do the talking since Ulysses will disdain the pilgrim's vulgar speech:

> Lascia parlare a me; ch'i'ho concetto
>   Ciò che tu vuoi. Chè sarebbero schivi,
> Perchè fuor Greci, forse del tuo detto.
> (*Inferno* XXVI, 73-75)

Only rhetoric speaks to rhetoric, and Jean-Baptiste's lofty language and rhetoric, as shown previously in the context of Nimrod, is characterized by a high frequency of disdain and pride. At this point, the text should also recall the language of Canto XXVI, as both succeed in masking the error of the sin.

To "preside over destinies" brings literally to mind Dante's Ulysses, the evil counselor, who presides over destinies, in the sense that he convinced his sailors to sail in the seemingly noble pursuit of "virtue and knowledge," thus leading them to their death through his perversion and persuasion of language. But there is not yet even enough context for one to establish if the destinies in question, regarding Camus's text, are those of sailors.

It is soon a matter once again of "disdain" in the *récit*. While its presence has proven to be applicable to other characters of the *Commedia*, it appears in conjunction with another mark of Ulysses:

> Je m'étonne parfois de l'obstination que met notre taciturne ami à bouder les langues civilisées.
> (p. 1477)

This is a direct echo and reversal of the situation as it appears in Canto XXVI of the *Inferno*: It is clear that Ulysses disdains the vulgar languages when Virgil says to the pilgrim:

> Lascia parlare a me; ch'i ho concetto
> Ciò che tu vuoi. Chè sarebbero schivi,
> Perchè fuor Greci, forse del tuo detto.
> (*Inferno* XXVI, 73-75)

This statement on the part of Jean-Baptiste is a most decisive one in the identification of Dante's Ulysses. Also, sirens, boats, and islands play a very marked role on the literal level of Clamence's words and the specificity required for Dante's character eventually makes itself known.

The first portion of the text reveals a first suggestion of circular motion, as Jean-Baptiste explains the suspicion of the barman:

> De là cet air de gravité ombrageuse, comme s'il avait le soupçon, au moins, que quelque chose ne tourne pas rond entre les hommes.
> (p. 1478)

Circular motion is of no literal concern in Ulysses' tale, but it is the perfect motion of the intellect which the souls of the *Inferno* have lost, and it is often imposed upon them: examples include Paolo and Francesca, caught literally in the "whirlwind of passion," Brunetto, running in circles under the rain of fire; or the hypocrites, finding themselves literally "gilded over," as they are condemned to walk slowly in circles. Perhaps the most famous example concerning circular motion is that of the Neutral Angels of the Vestibule of the *Inferno*: having refused to take sides in the quarrel between God and Lucifer, they are now forced to run in circles after a banner. Ulysses clearly lacks the perfect motion of the intellect which all the souls of his canticle have lost. Dante's pilgrim will reach that point where circle equals line.[2] On the other hand, Ulysses makes the error of equating virtue with science and knowledge.[3] Jean-Baptiste will literally dwell upon virtue, knowledge, and eventually and precisely his assimilation and rupture of the circle as follows:

> Le cercle dont j'étais le centre se brisait
> et ils se plaçaient sur une seule rangée. . . .
> (p. 1515)

Such a lack of synthesis implies loss of vision of the incarnation, of unity, etc... However, the geometrical language of *La Chute* becomes more and more visible with the *récit*'s progress. Lansing similarly notes of the *Paradiso* that the "souls of the *Paradiso* configure themselves in patterns of increasingly geometrical perfection."[4] Circles do not belong any more to Dante's *Inferno* than to the *Paradiso*: for example, in the latter's sphere of Mercury, the outline of a circle is formed as the souls are compared to fish rising to the surface to eat in a movement which emphasizes the natural hunger or desire of these souls. Fish in the process of eating form one of the memorable images of *La Chute*, and one must keep in mind that all elements of *La Chute* which could be a mark of the *Paradiso* or the *Purgatorio* are contaminated either by an ironic distance, an infernal element, and or an infernal context--as in the following:

> Quand je m'occupais d'autrui, c'était pure condescendance. . . . [J]e montais d'un degré dans l'amour que je me portais.
> (p. 1500)

The question of condescending, love, or climbing by degrees, imitates the language of the *Paradiso*, but Clamence contaminates this vocabulary through his self-centered goals and perceived meaning. Another example of such a process takes place in the following lines:

> [C]es minuscules poissons qui s'attaquent . . .
> au nageur . . . le nettoient . . . n'en laissant
> qu'un squelette immaculé.
> (p. 1479)

On the subject of circles, one should glance at the literal level of Canto III of the *Inferno*'s Vestibule, particularly as the latter is surprisingly identified during the course of *La Chute*, nonetheless in conjunction with "Dante." Camus literally asks his client if he is familiar with Dante and at the same time announces that we are located in the Vestibule. A closer look at Canto III of the *Inferno* reveals a surprising coincidence between its own vocabulary and the vocabulary of *La Chute*. Elements of the third canto which concern the rewriting include the "langues étranges," the "filer," the "tourner sans trêve," the "lueur vermeille cuivrée," the image of "la tête ceinte," the autumn leaves, the stench of the dead leaves, the "enseignes," the "mépris," the "sectes," the desire of these souls to cross, and the final "je chus" as the pilgrim faints.[5] However, the ruling factor is multiplicity with regard to *Canti* and canticles:

> [T]he *Divine Comedy*, as a whole, not merely the part called the *Inferno*, is important for an understanding of what lies ahead of the Fall.[6]

It is evident that foreign languages belong just as clearly to Nimrod's isotope as to Canto III of the *Inferno*. The literal elements of Canto III, the Vestibule, find themselves in high frequency in the first pages of Clamence's *récit*. He speaks to his client of "sectes" at length (p. 1480), of people whose heads appear separated from their bodies in the recurrent image of "leurs têtes dans cette brume de néon" (p. 1482), of "enseignes" in high frequency (pp. 1482, 1499, 1513), of people "filant rêveusement" and "tournant sans trêve" (p. 1482), of suspicion, of the "lumière dorée, cuivrée" (p. 1482), of the wish to cross the sea in the context of boats, sirens, and islands (p. 1483); and one should remind oneself that the above examples are not so rare, but regenerate themselves within *La Chute* as well as within Camus's other works. Autumn leaves also play a literal role in the *récit* as does their stench (pp. 1489 and 1497); but it is evident that this language is not restricted to the *Inferno* nor to a specific canto or character of Dante's poem: for example, decapitation plays the most clearly identifiable role in the realization of John the Baptist's isotope, but it could just as well apply to the souls of the Vestibule with their "tête ceinte," to the decapitated Bertrand de Born, or even to Justinian with his head hidden by the light. (André Pézard examines the character in terms of the symbol of the Flame.) One should also note that Justinian occupies two *canti* of the *Paradiso*, and that he, like Clamence, uses the *couper* formula. Most conclusive, however, is the coincidence between the Vestibule and particularly the last passage of the first part of the *récit* (pp. 1482-1483), leading to the identification of the Vestibule as a motivating force, since repetition and density of elements pertaining to the Vestibule play such marked roles. Such an identification is not destructive to Clamence's own identification in these very same pages of the "dernier

cercle," nor to the strong suggestion of Dante's rain of fire
(Canti XIV and XV), nor to the *Inferno* in general as present
in the everlasting "pregione etterna" and realm of "la morte
poesì" (*Purgatorio* I, 7). All this vocabulary plays an important role in *La Chute* which allows for such multiplicity, especially as all of its classifications are oscillating states,
in the sense that they define the Vestibule as well as other
circles and even canticles. Jean-Baptiste will literally have
to force himself to take sides (p. 1498), just as Dante's
Neutral Angels are forced to run after a banner for they know
not what reason. There is no correction or change in *La Chute*,
or in the *Inferno*, and immobilization is the pervading factor;
but while the *Inferno* is the dominant force in *La Chute*, the
Vestibule, the last circle, the *Paradiso*, the *Purgatorio*, Ulysses,
Ugolino, and any of the *canti* to come forth through the isotopes of the rewriting--all interconnect to produce irony in
La Chute and thematic continuity and correction in the *Commedia*.

Keeping in mind the range of associations, let us now return to the identification of Ulysses within the first portion
of the *récit*: for example, "Ulysses" is present in the three
canticles[7] and in practically endless thematic and literal
echoes of his own account of what happened, as told in Canto
XXVI of the *Inferno*: the flight, the madness, the desert shore,
the sea-going voyage and the expression in terms of a flight,
sirens, islands, shores, and "error" and its correction are
repeated elements throughout the three canticles.

In the second paragraph of the *récit*, the "host"'s job is described:

> Son métier consiste à recevoir des marins de toutes les nationalités. . . .
> (p. 1477)

The "sailors" confirm one step further the realization of the Ulysses isotope.

The next lines stress "exile," previously examined in the context of Nimrod, following the references to the tower of Babel, alienation, and the path that could evoke the anti-hero:

> Mais non, celui-ci ne sent pas son exil, il va son chemin, rien ne l'entame.
> (p. 1477)

Exile applies to so many characters of the *Commedia* as well as to Dante and to Camus; in the context of Ulysses, one recalls that Dante created his character to break all family, patriotic and human ties in his pursuit of the infinite--the very thing that destroyed him (in Dante's account), as the sea literally closed over him:

> Infin ch'il mar fu sopra noi richiuso.
> (*Inferno* XXVI, 142)

The above element, as an echo of the end point of the *Commedia* or narrative element of the story Dante creates, will also reproduce itself at *La Chute*'s end point. Dante places the hero among the Fraudulent of Malebolge in the circle of the Evil Counselors, and Ulysses finds himself hidden inside a double flame or "double tongue of fire," which moves as he speaks, and one never sees him. He shares the punishment with Diomedes, his accomplice to the theft of the Palladium. While his sin is that of having perverted language, it is for the theft of the image of Pallas (a blasphemous theft--blasphemy reuniting the categories subject to the symbol of the flame)[8] that Virgil identifies him to Dante-pilgrim:

> E del Palladio pena vi si porta.
> (*Inferno* XXVI, 63)

It is in the preceding canto that the thieves are punished; regarding Vanni Vucci, Pézard writes:

> C'est qu'au vol Vanni Fucci a joint le sacrilège: il a dérobé dans la chapelle Saint-Jacques au dome de Pistoi certaines reliques, moins précieuses par leur vêtement d'or et de gemmes que par leurs vertus spirituelles, et les vases sacrés où habite le Seigneur; ce trésor, il l'a mis en gage chez un usurier, par l'entreprise d'un prêtre plus que simoniaque. Comme pour mieux justifier cette peine du feu, la tirade de Vanni Fucci s'achève par un violent blasphème accompagné d'un geste obscène à la face de Dieu.[9]

Pézard examines the unifying thread where the symbol of the flame is concerned, and Dante's Vanni Fucci could very well reveal himself in the rewriting, under Dante's rain of fire along with the usurers and Brunetto Latini; under the symbol of the flame with the simoniacs and their feet in flames; or even Justinian with his head hidden in the divine light. (Pézard includes all these in his discussion of the symbol of the flame.)

Immediately following the reference to exile, the subject turns to the mouth, evoking the same dehumanization and distortion which occurs in the Ulysses scene (and soon to concretize itself):

> Une des rares phrases que j'aie entendues de sa
> bouche proclamait que c'était à prendre ou à
> laisser.
> (p. 1477)

The third paragraph of the *récit* reveals an empty space on the wall:

> Voyez par exemple, au-dessus de sa tête, sur
> le mur de fond, ce rectangle vide qui marque
> la place d'un tableau décroché. Il y avait
> là, en effet, un tableau et particulièrement
> intéressant, un vrai chef-d'oeuvre.
> (p. 1478)

The emphasis upon a missing art object, in proximity to the continued stress on the "head" of the barman, puts the reader on the track towards the Palladium, or perhaps even towards Vanni Fucci's sacred treasure, the theft, and its sacred nature, and the fact that Jean-Baptiste will identify himself as an accomplice to the crime and as a counselor. At present, the reference to the empty space on the wall no longer allows one possibly to dismiss the elements of the rewriting as purely archetypal, biblical, or as disjointed analogies: they clearly contribute to the formation of the isotope of Dante's Ulysses.

Since the "error," as the going off course towards the siren, is traditionally equated with that space within which poetic flights of language take place, it is not surprising that Jean-Baptiste's very own flights include digressions. Just as much of a digression is the way in which the literal or disfigured meaning of a word is mythologized to engender the language of the *récit*, and this process is made all the more evident to the reader of the rewriting, whether it becomes clear through repetition or through the isotopes. Elements of the process include the "rain," forever present on the literal level of Jean-Baptiste's *récit*, as well as in Camus's previous writings. Even the moment at which the rain stops is of utmost importance in *La Chute*. (The same formula of language which announces the rain is found again in Camus's previous works.) Such mythologization is a mark of Camus's writings (the author is conscious of the process)[10] and likewise of the inverted and literal world of the *Inferno*. Rain, elevation, blindness, mold, decapitation, fire, and immobilization are a few among the numerous elements to be disfigured through the isotopes of writing.

Let us proceed to examine the presence of Ugolino, as he is guilty of the sort of cannibalism to which the rewriting makes the reader an accomplice. Ugolino reverses the signs of Christianity; since eating is an interpretive act, people who read literally are cannibals. Since the rewriting is based on the literal deformation and resulting reversals, it is no surprise that Ugolino makes a lasting appearance in the text of *La Chute*--that is, if the deformations in question are legitimate. Ugolino is guilty of Compound fraud, the perversion of a bond, finds himself in the last circle and immobilized in the ice, and shares his canto with the Treacherous Hosts. The literal level of his account stresses the mouth, hunger, food, and tears, especially in the inability to cry due to the freezing conditions; the latter is of very high frequency in the canto.[11] As Ugolino lifts his head from the "fiero pasto" (*Inferno* XXXIII, 1), all emphasis is on the mouth, and he begins the tale which reveals the monstrous parody of Word made Flesh. Sinclair remarks that this is the longest of episodes in the *Inferno* and that "'silence and immobility take part as in no other episode' (Casini-Barbi)"[12] and qualifies this as one of those famous monologues which makes the sin forgotten; this one is characterized by "dreams, the sound of nails at the door, and the last days of stony despair and death, and the father blind, dying . . . and bearing . . . all the energy of his hate. . . ."[13]

Discomfort, voracious hunger, hate, exile in a tower, Ugolino having found himself eternally bound to the man who sealed him in the "Tower of Hunger" to starve,[14] now (in the *Inferno*) gnawing at the archbishop's head, the head, blindness, the tears, the mouth, prison cells, locked doors, sacrifice, dreams, bondage, treachery, and friendship--all play important roles in Camus's text rewritten. Since Ugolino is literally attached to Ruggieri, one should add the use of *s'accrocher* and *collé* in *La Chute* at several instances, and they prove meaningful as far as the Dantesque isotopes are concerned. Perhaps one can even to so far as to include the use of "s'essuyer," since Ugolino literally has to wipe his mouth from the savage feast before he is able to speak.[15] Similarly, the frequent *étranges courbatures* and *coincé* of the *récit* could well be indicators of Ugolino, or other infernal characters. The two texts share an insistance upon cold and physical immobilization. Jean-Baptiste finds himself progressively confined physically, just as the language of the rewriting is progressively immobilizing and immobilized. The structure is found in many of Camus's other works as in "Jonas ou l'artiste au travail" in *L'Exil et le royaume*; throughout so many of Camus's previous works, the roles of rooms, prison cells, and lying down, form a structural tendency towards immobilaztion, ending ultimately in death. In *La Chute*, the progression becomes concretized as, for example, in the passage from the third person usage *couché* to the more frequent usage by the first person. It is in the sixth and final part of the text that Jean-Baptiste assimilates the term:

> Je suis confus de vois recevoir couché.
> (p. 1537)

Among the above elements, hunger, sacrifice, the head, and the mouth, clearly apply to John the Baptist's isotope, but Dante's Ugolino is clearly present in them also. He could very well be behind lines such as:

> Une des rares phrases que j'air entendues de
> sa bouche proclamait que c'était à prendre ou
> à laisser. Que fallait-il prendre ou laisser?

In the context of the tower and exile, the juxtaposition of the mouth and silence to the ambiguity of language[16] supports the hypothesized presence of Ugolino. On the following page, "chewing" already enters into play, and will be of increasing importance with the progress of the *récit*. The use of "nourrir" is unexpected concerning what the barman does with his afterthoughts. He continues to "ruminate" (p. 1478). Jean-Baptiste then remarks "le goût du linge fin" in conjunction with words: "Le style, comme la popeline, dissimule trop souvent de l'eczéma" (p. 1478). This extensive language anchors itself in the expression of eating while it stresses the words themselves, dissimulation, and symbolic and religious language--all elements of Ugolino's Canto XXXIII.

In the subsequent comment upon history, Jean-Baptiste describes the methodical liquidation of people, while insisting on the mouth and fish, which again confirms the problematic language and cannibalism of Ugolino's tale, if one allows for the personification of such fish in "les petites bouchées rapides" (p. 1479) and "les petites dents qui s'attaquent à la chair" (p. 1479). Clamence comes to describe himself as being devoured (p. 1515), which traces the first person assimilation of language once again. Other marks of the religious and symbolic discourse are found in the repeated *repêcher*, concerning the saving of a drowning victim, and *pêcheurs* of the *récit*.

It is at the end of the first part of the *récit* that the people of Amsterdam are described as "coincé dans un petit espace," an expression which is soon followed by the use of "s'accrocher" and the "étranges courbatures" due to the cold. Ugolino's presence and situation are still suggested in such language, and particularly as the final identification of the "last circle" or Cocytus is made in this very portion of the work. Besides, these elements become increasingly evident with its progress, whether through repetition, literal contamination, or the realization of isotopes; they point to a double immobilization, the character's (whether or not Ugolino) as well as the general petrification of language. Ugolino will be undoubtedly present by Camus's final passage, as Jean-Baptiste will have dwelled on the fact of being "locked" in a room, "tied" to his fellow human beings, blindness, tears, his eventual physical immobilization, and other precise terms of the isotope; and in the final and ambiguous language, he insists upon the literal meaning of words, on religious and symbolic language, and the ambiguity of such language--all leading the reader to take him literally. Specificity allows one to conclude the underlying presence of Dante's character.

To the above, one should add the general climate of Clamence's words, which always focus upon themselves and problems in interpretation, along with the fact that almost all the isotopes of the rewriting converge upon the speaker: it is always Jean-Baptiste who mirrors and realizes the narrative and descriptive threads despite himself--that is, with no respect for time and place, even to the point of disregarding his own expressed personal likes and dislikes: everything takes place in the language and in the diegesis of the text. The speaker's own intention, powerless, only goes to prove the language of *La Chute* as a destiny.

Jean-Baptiste's language is laden with symbolic and poetic usage, and it succeeds in creating its own symbols as it mythologizes itself through repetition, odd juxtapositions and thought processes. The text alone even often revolves around certain words, their literal meanings, and associations. The insistance, for example, on the animal nature of the barman lends a meaning beyond the ridiculous. The insistence on Mexico-City, both visually (italics) and in meaning (out of place), results in the same duality and mythopoetic capacity. The same thing occurs regarding the *genièvre*, the *mépris*, the *enseignes*, the fish, the metallic glow and light, the *lessive*, and any of those elements whose disfigurement is confirmed by the literal level through the concept of the rewriting or even within the text's own coherence, as in the passing mention of locusts which gives way to further commentary.

The resulting duality does away with the distinctions between language as parody and language as revelation, in other words between the language of the *Inferno* and the language of the *Paradiso*. Another important example of this process of mythologization concerns the "rumination" (p. 1478) followed by matters of judgement, cleanliness, camels, hooves (fingernails), and Scripture. "Rumination" is followed by:

> Je sais bien que le goût du linge fin ne suppose pas forcément qu'on ait les pieds sales. N'empêche. Le style, comme la popeline, dissimule trop souvent de l'eczéma.
> (p. 1478)

The *juge-pénitent* proceeds to dwell even further on cleanliness, justice, and a washing which easily brings to mind either the cleansing of the *Purgatorio* or, more precisely, an inverted purging process--inverted in the sense that a language which evokes the *Purgatorio* (or *Paradiso*) turns to corruption:

> Vous avez entendu parler, naturellement, de ces miniscules poissons des rivières brésiliennes qui s'attaquent au nageur imprudent, le

> nettoient . . . n'en laissant qu'un squelette
> immaculé? Eh bien, c'est ça leur organisation.
> Voulez-vous d'une vie propre? . . . On va vous
> nettoyer. . . . [C]'est à qui nettoiera l'autre.
> (p. 1479)

Soon thereafter, Clamence reveals the matter of judgement and the presence of a "camel" as well as "hooves:"

> Il faut me consentir un peu de raffinement.
> Le chameau qui a fourni le poil de mon pardessus souffrait sans doute de la gale; en revanche, j'ai les ongles faits.
> (p. 1480)

In Canto XIV of the *Purgatorio*, Dante's use of rumination occurs in the context of judgement and cleanliness, from the Mosaic laws regarding the cleanliness of ruminating animals with cloven hooves: the camel ruminates but does not have cloven hooves, therefore he is unfit for human consumption. By extension, lack of cloven hooves equals a lack of distinctions, therefore a lack of justice. In this context, Dante's words can evoke so clearly the language of Camus's judge.[17] *La Chute*'s subject matter becomes very religious in the context of a cleansing sea (the recurrent *lessive*) to arrive at passages such as the following, which insists upon Scripture:

> Les professions m'intéressent moins que les
> sectes. Permettez-moi de vous poser deux questions et n'y répondez que si vous ne les jugez
> pas indiscrètes. Possédez-vous des richesses?
> Quelques-unes? Bon. Les avez-vous partagées
> avec les pauvres? Non. Vous êtes donc ce que
> j'appelle un saducéen. Si vous n'avez pas pratiqué les Ecritures, je reconnais que vous n'en
> serez pas plus avancé. Cela vous avance? Vous
> connaissez donc les Ecritures?
> (p. 1480)

In the same line of thought, the making of distinctions is a constant factor of *La Chute*'s literal level. Jean-Baptiste repeatedly makes statements incorporating the *couper au jugement* formula (pp. 1478, 1487, 1514, and 1522).

Therefore history, judgement, Scripture, nails or hooves, rumination, cutting or making distinctions, cleanliness, and the camel form a tightly knit complex of language. Once again in the context of the literal deformation of words, the camel hair coat worn by Clamence (p. 1480) and his clean fingernails (p. 1480) are sure marks, especially in such proximity, of the process. To these, one should add the high frequency of *couper*, which leads the reader to a literal separation, announcing the fall of language, and the final decapitation: in such images as those which result from this language, it again becomes clear that the language of poetry and revelation collapses with a language which is conscious of itself as medium.

At the same time that the above complex network of associations functions, it is evident that the camel hair dress is a symbol of penitence for John the Baptist. Also isotopic elements of his presence include the giving up of worldly goods, the desert, locusts, and decapitation. The patron saint of Florence is an obvious engendering presence throughout the *récit*; but, while elements such as laughter, the camel dress, the desert, doves, and Elijah work perfectly well in terms of John the Baptist's isotope, they also apply to other situations and structures. "Laughter," for example, is a

highly frequent element of Dante's Earthly Paradise at the end
of the *Purgatorio*. In *La Chute*, "laughter" appears in conjunction with the references to summits, loss of memory, and the
Vert Galant's garden of Clamence's island-summit, evoking the
Earthly Paradise at the peak of the *Purgatorio*'s island-mount.
Loss of memory evokes clearly the river Lethe, and the garden
evokes the garden. Regarding other elements listed above,
Jacqueline Lévi-Valensi writes:

> D'un bout à l'autre de son récit, Clamence ne
> cessera de jouer son rôle et la personnalité
> de celui à qui il emprunte son nom et quelque
> peu de son language et de sa situation. Madame
> Adèle King remarque fort justement que Clamence
> 'est vêtu comme Jean-Baptiste. . . . Il s'appelle lui-même un prophète criant dans le désert. Comme Jean-Baptiste, il se compare à
> Elie, et il tente de faire descendre les colombes. . . .'18

While the above is evident, one recalls that elements such as
"Elie" are significant in the Ulysses episode. Descending
doves are an important symbol of the Francesca da Rimini episode and act as a symbol for the whole of its canticle, as
well as in the subsequent two. Similarly, the camel hair coat
plays a role outside of John the Baptist's presence.

Let us now return to the literal concretion of Ulysses
in the following deformation of the "sirènes du port"--a deformation permitted by the juxtaposition of a path, the sirens'
tempting call, the port, and the "music" in final position:

> [E]ntendez-vous les sirènes du port? Votre
> chemin... Eh bien... Mais verriez-vous un
> inconvénient, ce serait le plus simple, à ce
> que je vous accompagne jusqu'au port? . . .

> Vous trouverez ces belles avenues où défilent
> des tramways chargés . . . de musiques. . . .
> (pp. 1480-1481)

Shortly after the above words are spoken, the expression of "ils écoutent les sirènes" is followed by "la navigation," and the final image of the *récit*'s first section:

> [L]es îles dérivent. . . .
> (p. 1483)

Even though the sirens, the music, the navigation, the islands, and the going off course to reach the inverted shipwreck, one in which the islands stray off course (instead of boats), thus announcing the immobility of Clamence's navigational discourse, all belong to *La Chute*'s own coherent literal level,[19] they clearly outline the call of the mythological siren. Even the last paragraph of the first part of the text, without the intervention of Dante's poem, is a siren's call to leave the world and go off the straight path. The female figure will succeed yet again in playing an important role in the principal event of Clamence's *récit*, nonetheless in the context of presumption, mountain tops, false flights, and other elements which mark the presence of Ulysses and his false arrival in the Earthly Paradise of the summit of the island of Purgatory.

The symbol of the flame[20] is a recurrent element of the *Commedia*, whether in the blasphemous categories of the *Inferno* or the corrected and divine light of the *Paradiso*. Ulysses is condemned to suffer in Malebolge (the "evil ditches" in which ten concentric ditches are connected by a series of stone dikes serving as bridges), and he is subject to confinement in the eternal double flame shared with his accomplice. Dante-pilgrim's descent to this zone follows his crossing of the plain subject to an eternal rain of fire (*Inferno* XIV and XV) which condemns the violent against God, nature, and art. This order of events probably leads nowhere with respect to the re-writing: it is the symbol of the flame which concerns us. In *La Chute*, Clamence presents the first of many passing references to "rain" (p.1481). The repetition, often in stressed positions (for example, at the beginning of a paragraph), is enough to transform it into a symbol, but its meaning is intensified through the rewriting as well as through Camus's previous works; most blatantly, in "Pluies de New York"[21]; in South America, in "La Pierre qui pousse"; in North Africa, in *La Peste*; in Paris and in Amsterdam, within *La Chute* itself. In the latter, Clamence even makes an issue of that instance at which it is no longer raining, and the same formula of language is found again in Camus's previous works:

> Tiens, la pluie a cessé.
> (p. 1511)

Clamence notices the rain has stopped when he remembers vividly the night a woman threw herself off a bridge over the Seine. Also in Dante's two *canti* dedicated to the rain of fire, the rain stops over the bridge as the pilgrim and Virgil begin their crossing. The bridge is located over Phlegyas, and the rain stops in order that the two travellers may pass unharmed. Phlegyas is a river of blood, and it so happens that Jean-Baptiste refers to "blood" during *La Chute*'s parallel incident, as he describes "un sang doux, comme la pluie tombait . . ." (p. 1413), thus leading to another strong suggestion of Camus's rain of fire as Dantesque in its origin and the symbol of the flame. According to Pézard, it extends to include Ulysses, Vanni Fucci, the thieves, Pope Nicholas, the Virtuous Heathens, and the Epicureans (and elements of the other two canticles); however, within *La Chute*, one expects the internal identities to be fragmented by elements of lyricism and revelation: the latter are transformed into the contaminating factors.

The same passage containing the first mention of "rain" in *La Chute* also emphasizes images of light, smoke, metals, green, gold, red, lack of color, its own lyricism, fog, and dreams. Too many of these elements typify the *Purgatorio* to dismiss the latter's presence, but smoke and dreams (Ugolino) obviously have their place in the *Inferno*; in the punishment of the thieves, who turn to ashes;[22] and under the rain of fire. Fog, the red glow of Dis, the green banner after which Ser Brunetto runs, and the gold of the tales of corruption (which include Pope Nicholas III) show such elements not to be necessarily suggestive of the *Purgatorio*. The ambiguity appears all the more justified as Jean-Baptiste admiringly and accusingly refers to washing and cleansing in the recurrent *lessive*; literal and figurative language merge together once again, along with the fact that Jean-Baptiste is about to identify the "last circle" of the *Inferno*:

> Tout ce monde, hein, si tard, et malgré la
> pluie, qui n'a pas cessé depuis des jours!
> Heureusement, il y a le genièvre, la seule lueur
> dans ces ténèbres. Sentez-vous la lumière dorée,
> cuivrée, qu'il met en vous? J'aime marcher
> à travers la ville, le soir, dans la chaleur
> du genièvre. Je marche des nuits durant, je
> rêve, ou je me parle interminablement. . . .
> J'aime, ce peuple grouillant sur les trottoirs,
> coincé dans un petit espace de maisons et
> d'eaux, cerné par des brumes, des terres froides,
> et la mer fumante comme une lessive. Je l'aime,
> car il est double. Il est ici et il est ail-
> leurs.
>
> (p. 1482)

In the above passage, darkness, rain, crowds, corruption, cold, gold, and the *coincé* suggest the presence of the *Inferno*; but the *sfumature* and twice occurring *cuivré* (see Pézard's note to *Purgatorio* XVIII, 76 on which the "copper" is a Dantesque addition to the biblical reference; also the recurrent "copper" of Camus's previous works), the cleansing, and the lyricism of these words belong most accurately to the *Purgatorio*. In the company of such details, the constant references made by Clamence to dreams, thirst, and the *genièvre* evoke the second canticle--the canticle of dreams, natural thirst and natural hunger, natural desire, and *sfumature*. Jean-Baptist's course of salvation is naturally always condemned to duplicity and irony, as it inversely succeeds in contaminating the infernal quality of his words.

A preliminary hint at Pope Nicholas III's underlying presence can also be seen in the above cited passage. These very same words also follow explicit references to the Dantesque categories of usurers (p. 1479), pimps (pp. 1479 and 1496), and prostitutes (pp. 1479 and 1483). But Pope

Nicholas II provides an extensive isotope which will prove most interesting in its specificity. Presently, in the juxtaposition of "coincé dans un petit espace" to the elements of gold and corruption and prostitution, the Pope is vaguely suggested. Placed in Canto XIX of the *Inferno*, he is guilty of having made a mockery of holy office and of having made a prostitute of the Church for his own personal gain. He finds himself placed upside down in a parody of the baptismal fonts of Florence's Cathedral San Giovanni, dedicated to the patron saint of that city, John the Baptist. Pope Nicholas is placed head first in a rocky hole with the soles of his feet in flames, and he is pushed further and further into the rocky crevices as his followers arrive at the same spot in the *Inferno*. (The use of *coincé* will provide us with the rewriting's most interesting case of increasing specificity.) Boniface is next to replace him. Another string of elements of Canto XIX, which will somewhat surface to *La Chute*'s literal level, is found in Dante's reference to having saved a drowning victim of the font by breaking it.[23] It is Pope Nicholas III's isotope which will prove to be the most exemplary of the rewriting process, insofar as it is neither archetypal nor Biblical and runs through a process of gradual concretion throughout the *récit* to converge eventually upon the speaker: as usual, he will realize the Dantesque presence with full disregard for place, real time (not the time of the story), and his own personal likes and dislikes. This isotope is clearly realized purely in the language of the *récit* and is uniquely Dantesque in identification.

In the final passages of the first part of the *récit*, the people of Amsterdam, as Camus's prophet sees them, are a guilty and wonderful crowd, giving way to infernal and lyrical language. Even if one prefers not yet to anticipate the presence of certain of the proposed categroies of Dante's system, Clamence has literally identified usurers, pimps, and prostitutes--all precise categories of sinners in Dante's *Inferno*. The usurers of the *Inferno* find themselves immobilized in a crouched position under the rain of fire. Sharing their plain, is Brunetto Latini, among the Sodomites (sodomy in having violated the nature of language) who runs a race in circles looking as if he belongs to the next group and guilty of having taught man "how to make himself eternal" through literature; he will also be somewhat of a concretized presence throughout the *récit*, but presently as vague as Pope Nicholas III, Ugolino, or the Neutral Angels. In any case, Clamence's attitude is positive and lyrical towards all these categories of possibly or precisely Dantesque sinners, as he confirms:

> Je l'aime, car il est double. Il est ici et
> il est ailleurs.
> (p. 1482)

The duplicity of the *Inferno* and the paradox of the *Paradiso* are literally working together. Clamence succeeds in adding poetry to his *Inferno*, as well as words of revelation and will even come to coin "le lyrisme cellulaire" (p. 1549), foreshadowed in his present words.

The next paragraph could suggest Ulysses' punishment, his head hidden inside the double flame shared with his silent accomplice to the theft of the Palladium. In Dante's Canto XXVI of the *Inferno*, two similes introduce the scene; "Elijah" will literally surface in Clamence's *récit*. The punishment is suggested in images of decapitation and light. Further along in the same passage, Ulysses' presence is confirmed in the literal presence of islands, error, flight, and madness. This same paragraph also contains "heavy steps" and circular motion, together suggesting Dante's hypocrites. The description of the people of Amsterdam also juxtaposes literature, eternal life, and continuous circular motion—all pointing to the presence of Dante's teacher, Brunetto Latini. Also present among these terms are the souls of the Vestibule. All elements of the presently vague Dantesque identities are present in Clamence's following (previously examined) words:

> Mais oui! A écouter leurs pas lourds, . . . à les voir passer pesamment entre leurs boutiques, pleines de harengs dorés et de bijoux couleur de feuilles mortes, vous croyez sans doute qu'ils sont là, ce soir? Vous . . . prenez ces braves gens pour une tribu de syndics et de marchands, comptant leurs écus avec leurs chances de vie éternelle, et dont le seul lyrisme consiste à prendre parfois . . . des leçons . . . ? Vous vous trompez. Ils marchent près de nous, il est vrai, et pourtant, voyez où se trouvent leurs têtes; dans cette brume de néon, de genièvre et de menthe qui descend des enseignes rouges et vertes. La Hollande est un songe, monsieur, un songe d'or et de fumée, plus fumeux le jour, plus doré la nuit, et nuit et jour ce songe est peuplé de Lohengrin comme ceux-ci, filant rêveusement sur leurs noirs bicyclettes à hauts guidons, cygnes funèbres qui tournent sans trêve, dans tout le pays, autour des mers, le long des canaux.

> Ils rêvent, la tête dans leurs nuées cuivrées,
> ils roulent en rond, ils prient, somnambules,
> dans l'encens doré de la brume, ils ne sont
> plus là. Ils sont partis à des milliers de
> kilomètres, vers Java, l'île lointaine. Ils
> prient ces dieux grimaçants . . . qui errent
> au-dessus de nous, avant de s'accrocher, comme
> des signes somptueux, aux enseignes et aux
> toits en escaliers, pour rappeler à ces colons
> nostalgiques que la Hollande n'est pas seule-
> ment l'Europe des marchands, mais la mer, la
> mer qui mène à Cipango, et à ces îles où les
> hommes meurent fous et heureux.
> (p. 1482)

With respect to the passages previously examined, it becomes clear that the concept of a gradual concretion is working through repetition, literal deformation, and density of the elements as they surface to the literal level of the *récit* in the realization of the Dantesque isotopes. Even within the above paragraph, an increase in the so-called density from beginning to end takes place. The last passage of the *récit*'s first portion (to follow the above) will confirm many suspicions. The paragraph preceding the above one contained "smoke," "gold," "copper," circular motion, rain, darkness, cold, and all the previously suggested Dantesque categories found either subject to excessive repetition or further realization in the above cited lengthy passage: for instance, those categories subjected to circular motion make at least the suggestion of a more concretized Dantesque existance in the "pas lourds," "pesamment," explicitly circular motion, and references to golden light--all pointing to the identification of Dante's hypocrites (not to mention the duplicity stressed throughout the *récit*'s own coherence). Circular motion, eternal life, and lyricism, and the fact of "taking lessons" point to the underlying presence of Ser Brunetto. Sharing the plain with Brunetto, the usurers, who literally made their appearance earlier in the *récit*, further realize their non-extensive isotope here. The Neutral Angels also come forth hesitantly in the interminable circular motion and choice of vocabulary. Likewise, a vocabulary which characterizes the *Inferno* exists in greater denisty here. Most undeniably present, Ulysses comes forth to the literal level with increasing density and specificity of applicable terms of his isotope: from the "disdain" of the "civilized languages," to the theft of an art object, to the "sirens," and to the suggestion of his punishment in the double flame, the paragraph presently in question arrives at that point where "error," flight and descent, "islands," "departure," the "sea," "madness," "death," and "happiness" trace a major part of his Dantesque journey. Furthermore, the language of this passage is the language of an "evil counselor," as Clamence inverts the reasoning. Let us also recall that Dante's Ulysses, representing the hero of an anti-voyage for Dante-pilgrim undertakes an unsuccessful sea-going voyage now expressed in terms of a successful flight--in the simile of Elijah, and consequently Camus's juxtaposition of "errer," in the flight of gods, to the descent, follows perfectly the course of error of Dante's character. Echoed in Clamence's discourse are perhaps Ulysses' most famous words:

> Dei remi facemmo ali al folle volo.
> (*Inferno* XXVI, 125)

The flight imagery takes control of the *récit*, and juxtaposed to the literally present madness, it tells again Ulysses' tale.

Through the listed examples, the literal deformation of the meaning of words to realize the isotopes is a clear requirement of the writing, justified in that it finds itself confirmed on the literal level. The gods who "errent au-dessus de nous" before descending and latching on to the infernal *enseignes* (present throughout the *récit* lend their action to a deformation, particularly as they fall with the "error," the "madness," the voyage, and the "islands," and so many specific elements within such proximity of one another, that Ulysses' underlying presence is undeniable. Besides, the image of gods descending occurs to a more literal extent a few pages later with "ces dieux que, de temps en temps, on descend, au moyen d'une machine, pour transfigurer l'action et lui donner son sens" (p. 1488). The most conclusive evidence of this process of literal concretion of the Dantesque presence, with respect to repetition, density, specificity, and mass, occurs in the final passage of the *récit*'s first portion. At least in terms of mass and density, this page is the most densely populated and lengthly rewritten segment of probably the whole *récit*:

> Pardonnez-moi, l'habitude, monsieur, la vocation, le désir, aussi où je suis de bien vous faire comprendre cette ville, et le cœur des choses!
> (pp. 1482-1483)

Since Clamence lives "sur les lieux d'un des plus grands crimes de l'histoire," the deformed *cœur* lends itself so easily to the identification of Cocytus, located at the very center of the Earth in Dante's configuration. The following repetition of the word suggests further the validity of the deformation:

> Car nous sommes au cœur des choses.
> (p. 1483)

Already the *cœur* has taken on a much more physical meaning, and its Dantesque significance is soon confirmed:

> Avez-vous remarqué que les canaux concentriques d'Amsterdam ressemblent aux cercles de l'enfer? L'enfer bourgeois, naturellement peuplé de mauvais rêves. Quand on arrive de l'extérieur, à mesure qu'on passe ses cercles, la vie, et donc ses crimes, devient plus épaisse, plus obscure. Ici, nous sommes dans le dernier cercle. Le cercle des... Ah! Vous savez cela? Diable, vous devenez plus difficile à classer. Mais vous comprenez alors pourquoi je puis dire que le centre des choses est ici, bien que nous nous trouvions à l'extrémité du continent.
> (p. 1483)

Every detail is accurate within Dante's configuration to include associations in language and thematics. As one passes through the concentric circles of the *Inferno*, the crimes become more and more serious in nature, and there is less and less light. The *Inferno* also is, at least to some degree, a system of classification, of which its *enseignes* are a sign. Also, in this passage, at that moment when Jean-Baptiste hesitates to finish his sentence attempting to categorize the client, one should anticipate the question of "classification." Even his figurative use of "Diable" and "obscure" lend themselves accordingly to the rewriting's deformations. In such literal terms, obviously the most conclusive factors of this passage are the references to the above within the "last circle." Within this context, the question of circles and the physical center literally take over the discourse. While all connotation is infernal, Clamence manages, as usual, to reverse all these signs--implying that classification saves and damns the soul. Likewise, the natural thirst for the *genièvre* is always aiming for duplicity in the contiguous and corresponding images of decapitation, Clamence qualifies the "greatest crime in history" as "admirable" (p. 1481), and "pleads" (p. 1483) a case in favor of his damned souls. Duplicity extends to its explicit expression in the last words of the above cited passage, in the coexistence of the "center" and the "extremity;" but, within the context of the rewriting, the logical step from the last circle is to the shore of the island-mount of Purgatory--or to the shore of the "dark wood" where Dante-pilgrim begins his journey, since both are points of landing following shipwreck (or "error") and contain literal echoes of one another and of Ulysses' voyage as invented by Dante. Clamence's own words continue to express the shipwreck, the "shore," the "siren," the "boat," and the island's shore:

> En tout cas, les lecteurs de journaux et les fornicateurs ne peuvent aller plus loin. Ils viennent de tous les coins de l'Europe et s'arrêtent autour de la mer intérieure, sur la grève décolorée. Ils écoutent les sirènes, cherchent en vain la silhouette des bateaux dans la brume, puis repassent les canaux et s'en retournent à travers la pluie. Transis, ils viennent demander, en toutes langues, du genièvre à *Mexico-City*. Là, je les attends.
> (p. 1483)

However, contrary to Ulysses' isotope, "les lecteurs et les fornicateurs" bring another subject into play, particularly as the exact juxtaposition of words occurred a few paragraphs earlier:

> Je rêve parfois de ce que diront de nous les historiens futurs. Une phrase leur suffira pour l'homme moderne: il forniquait et lisait des journaux.
> (p. 1479)

Chiampi, in his discussion of the Francesca da Rimini episode, refers to their sin and punishment with respect to the sin as previously worded in Saint Augustine's *Confessions*:

> I was tossed and spilled floundering in the broiling sea of my fornication and you said no word. I deserted you and allowed myself to be carried away by the sweep of the tide.[24]
> (pp. 43-44, II, 2)

Paolo and Francesca will also concretize their presence during the course of the *récit*, and Jean-Baptiste, as usual, will assimilate and realize their isotope, and accordingly condemn himself in terms of salvation.

The "last circle" or "interior sea" evoke clearly the inner lake of Cocytus and happen to be spoken at that moment when Clamence makes his second reference to the diversity of languages at Mexico-City. Along with the "frozen to the bone" of "transis," the literal elements of this passage surely do more than suggest Cocytus and an imperfect anagram in the name of the bar. The "inner sea" is followed by the "shore," then "sirens," then "boats," then "fog," and finally the crossing back to *Mexico-City*. In this case, the order validates our interpretation of these elements in terms of the rewriting.

Whether the shore is that of the *Inferno*'s Canto I or that of the *Purgatorio*'s Canto I, it makes no difference; a backwards movement is traced with respect to the *Commedia*, and is therefore a fall. No crossing is possible. The validity of the deformation of the "sirens" is once and for all permitted by the context and the high frequency of literally infernal elements.

In the next lines, Jean-Baptiste anticipates the shipwreck or plunge expected if there is no shore at which to cross. In spite of his language, the survival of the shipwreck, which occurs for Dante-pilgrim, is not going to take place for Jean-Baptiste:

> Supposez, après tout, que quelqu'un se jette
> à l'eau. De deux choses l'une, ou vous l'y
> suivez pour le repêcher et, dans la saison
> froide, vous risquez le pire! Ou vous l'y
> abandonnez et les plongeons rentrés laissent
> parfois d'étranges courbatures.
> (p. 1483)

The plunge or fall, as stated above, will be verbally echoed in *La Chute*'s very last words, and the parallel syntax contains the expression of a real plunge. One recalls the use of "s'accrocher" following the flight of gods (p. 1482), which suggests the punishment inflicted upon Paolo and Francesca in the whirlwind, as they are unable to come down. By extension, one should note any of those punishments which impose eternal circular motion upon the sinner. Similarly, one should include the assimilating force of the "last circle" and of Jean-Baptiste: whether omnipresent in the impossibility of a crossing and the turning back from a shore, or in the literal contamination of numerous elements, the "last circle" is always the destiny, just as Jean-Baptiste, situated in the "center of things," finds himself most often the ruling force and end point, in the realization of the rewriting's isotopes. The resulting immobility, whether the concretion evolves through repetition or, more convincingly, gradually increasing density and specificity of elements, is the mark of a fall and inversion. Even the doves of *La Chute* wish to descend, like the doves of Canto V of the *Inferno*; the canto of Paolo and Francesca is an emblem of desire for the whole of the *Inferno*. While the three dove images of the *Commedia* reveal a progression, there is no change in the three dove images of the *récit*. Doves, in themselves, are certainly not indicative of Dante's *Commedia*, but given the context of the rewriting and the elements that have already shown themselves to be working, one can surely allow for the Dantesque interpretation.

The last few lines of the first part of the *récit* express the call of a siren to go off course accompanied by the lyrical element, the metaphorically stressed sea-going voyage, the departure and isolation from the human world (dreams, windows, and curtains), a descent suggesting flight, islands, and going off course (this version of a shipwreck); they dictate the inevitable plunge:

> Comment? Ces dames derrière les vitrines? Le rêve, monsieur, le rêve à peu de frais, le voyage aux Indes. Ces personnes se parfument aux épices. Vous entrez, elles tirent les rideaux et la navigation commence. Les dieux descendent sur les corps nus et les îles dérivent. . . .
> (p. 1483)

In their entirety, the above words express a call to leave the world, and also a female invitation to begin the navigation that ends in shipwreck; thus, Ulysses' tale is further realized, even if it is the "islands" which "go off course."

Once again, the impossibility of crossing to the shore, which marks the survival of Ulysses' shipwreck, illustrates Clamence's ability to turn immobility into movement and confuse duplicity with paradox. The true subject of such lyrical words, even within the text's own coherence, is an invitation by the "evil counselor" to pursue the island where he will never arrive, perhaps even incorporating the "palm tree" as an inverted pine or symbol of John the Baptist to the *Purgatorio*'s gluttonous:

> Les dieux descendent sur les corps nus et les
> îles dérivent, démentes, coiffées d'une cheve-
> lure ébouriffée de palmiers sous le vent.
> Essayez.
>   (p. 1483)

The few pages that constitute the *récit*'s first portion have revealed isotopes of the rewriting to be working with gradually increasing density and gradually increasing Dantesque specificity to a lesser extent. The literal level of Jean-Baptiste's *récit* leads to that point where references to "concentric circles" and "the last circle" support so strongly the rewriting's validity. In a parallel movement, the specificity of Ulysses' isotope emerged, from possible intertextual hints to isotopic formation, a pattern which becomes so striking in the remainder of Clamence's words. For now, there remain many of those vague intertextual hints of which many have already begun to succumb (to different degrees) to the centrifugal force that leads to the concretion of the rewriting's isotopes; others will progress no further. Such valid proof, as already demonstrated and in light of what is to come, reveals undeniable structural progressions; thus, the pattern is one of synthesis. In keeping with this concept, Jean-Baptiste reflects the movement of his discourse in his ability to absorb isotopes and intertextual references; he will even absorb the "shipwreck" within himself, as he speaks of islands:

>   [J]e dérive, moi aussi. . . . Arrêtez-moi. . . .
>   (*La Chute*, p. 1525)

He will realize isotopes begun by others (the third person) to include Ugolino, Paolo and Franesca, Ser Brunetto, and Pope Nicholas--all present in the *récit* to varying degrees. This capacity to assimilate isotopic elements to the first person of the *récit* takes place with a total disregard for time, place, and Clamence's relationship to the third person at the origin of the narrative and descriptive thread. In the absorption of the isotope, Jean-Baptiste equates himself with a center point or Cocytus when, after having literally identified the zone, he states:

>   Là, je les attends.
>   (p. 1483)

In such a context, he could evoke either Nimrod, Ugolino, a Treacherous Host, or Lucifer, frozen at Cocytus' center. Since Jean-Baptiste, more than other characters of the *récit*, carries out the realization of the rewriting process to its fullest extent, it is no surprise that reflections become more and more a part of his language in the process of self-accusation he has designed. It is a logical result that, at the end of his fully spoken account Jean-Baptiste echoes syntactically such a decisive moment as the perhaps most massive, dense, and specifically rewritten one (p. 1483), literally refers to his client as his mirror image. After all, increasing reflections are a principal mark of the *Paradiso*, and therefore, as one approaches a supposed moment of revelation, it is very ironic that Clamence juxtaposes such language of the beatific vision to the fall, plunge, and suicide. The resulting separation is announced all the way through the *récit*, beginning with the "here and elsewhere," the heads in the neon clouds of metallic light, and the language which confuses so clearly the language of the *Inferno* with the language of poetry and the cleansing or purging process and the language of the *Paradiso* with its paradox and reflection and revelation.

Footnotes to Chapter III

[1] *Purgatorio* I, 7.

[2] In John Freccero's "Dante's Ulysses; from Epic to Novel," in *Concepts of the Hero in the Middle Ages and The Renaissance*, Papers of the fourth and fifth annual conference of the Center for Medieval and Early Renaissance Studies, Ed. Norman T. Burns and Christopher J. Reagan (Albany State University: New York Press, 1975), pp. 101-119; Freccero writes that the unity of the poem is based on a new view of linearity with respect to time, the point where circle is line, the point where poet and pilgrim, the end point of the *Commedia*, and a vision of the incarnation. In Freccero's article, he also refers to St. Augustine's statement in "All the circles have been shattered," as a mark of that "new linearity with respect to time" and a synthesis of the epic as circular, and the novel as linear. (p. 165).

[3] "'Considerate la vostra semenza:/Fatti non foste a viver come brute,/Ma per seguir virtute e canoscenza.'" (*Inferno* XXVI, 118-120).

[4] Richard H. Lansing, "Patterns of Meaning: Similes in a Series," in *From Image to Idea: A Study of the Simile in Dante's "Commedia"* (Ravenna: Longo Editore, 1976), p. 157.

[5] I have used a French translation so as to make the correspondence clearer: André Pézard, Trans. and comments, *Dante: oeuvres complètes* (Paris: Gallimard, Bibliothèque de la Pléiade, 1965).

[6] Alfred Cordes, *The Descent of the Doves: Camus's Journey to the Spirit* (Washington, D.C.: University Press of America, 1980).

[7] *Inferno* XXVI and XXVII; *Purgatorio* XIX, 22; *Paradiso* XXVII, 82 ff.

[8] André Pézard, *Dante sous la pluie de feu*, pp. 288-290.

[9] Ibid., p. 289.

[10] Camus states that an image, like a symbol, has "une valeur de miracle" (Albert Camus, *L'Envers et l'endroit* [Paris: Gallimard, 1958] p. 113); "Melville a construit ses symboles sur le concret, non dans le matériau du rêve. Le créateur de mythes ne participe au génie que dans la mesure où il les inscrit dans l'épaisseur de la réalité et non dans les nuées fugitives de l'imagination" (Idem., "Herman Melville," in *Théâtre, récits, nouvelles*, p. 1909); Camus states that myth is to

religion what poetry is to truth (Idem., "*L'Eté* Paris: Gallimard, livre de poche, 1959, p. 59).

11 "'. . . /Parlare e lacrimar vedrai inseme (*Inferno* XXXIII, 9);" . . . /Pianger senti' fra 'l sonno i miei figliuoliñch'eran con meco, e domandar del pane" (Ibid., 38-39); "Io non piangea, si dentro impetrai:/Piangevan elli . . ." (Ibid., 49-50); "Percio non lacrimai . . . " (Ibid., 52); "Lo pianto stesso li pianger non lascia,/E 'l duol, che truova in su li occhi rintoppo,/ Si volge in entro a far crescer l'ambascia;/Chè le lagrime prime fanno groppo,/E sì come visiere di cristallo,/Riempion sotto 'l ciglio tutto il coppo" (Ibid., 94-99).

12 Quoted in Sinclair, *Dante's "Inferno"*, pp. 415-416.

13 Ibid., pp. 415-416.

14 Ugolino was incarcerated with his two sons. . . . After some months the door of their jail was nailed up, and they were left to starve" (C. H. Grandgent, ed. and annotator, "*La divina commedia*" *di Dante Alighieri* [Boston: D. C. Heath and Company, 1933], p. 295).

15 "La bocca sollevò dal fiero pasto/Quel peccator forbendola a' capelli/Dal capo ch' elli avea di retro guasto" (*Inferno* XXXIII, 1-3).

16 "'Poscia, più che il dolor, potè 'l digiuno'" (Ibid. 75); "After some months the door of their jail was nailed up, and they were left to starve. When their bodies were taken out, several days after their death, they were found to be badly rat bitten; and a couple of old chroniclers declare that the unfortunate prisoners had eaten one another's flesh. . . . It was perhaps a desire to explain the mutilation in a more fitting way that led Dante to conceive of Ugolino, in his intolerable anguish, as gnawing his own hands. Nevertheless some modern commentators have imagined that Dante intended, in the last verse of Ugolino's speech, to imply that the bereaved father was driven to cannibalism" (Grandgent, "*La divina Commedia*" *di Dante Alighieri*, p. 295).

17 "Le leggi son, ma chi pon mano ad esse?/ Nullo però che 'l pastor che procede,/ruminar può, ma non ha l'unghie fesse" (*Purgatorio* XVI, 97-99); Also see the emperor Justinian, who put the eagle, or set the course of history, back in the right direction; regarding law, he too "cuts" them (*Paradiso* VI, 12); one recalls that the laughter put the "order back into things" for Clamence.

18 Jacqueline Lévi-Valensi, "*La Chute* ou la parole en procès," in *La Revue des lettres modernes*, Nos. 238-244 (1970), pp. 33-57.

[19] Likewise, such terms as the *dériver* of the *récit* are assimilated by Clamence's first person discourse, once again confirming the immobility as destiny, and that such important factors as these trace their importance most clearly through the rewriting.

IV.

Isotopic Concretions and Assimilations

In the second part of the *récit*, Jean-Baptiste begins by telling his history, before the conversion--that is, the events which lead up to his "brusque volte-face" on the bridge over the Seine. The latter supposedly changed his life and leads, through literal echoes, to the existence of two other parallel events. The original, in terms of historical time, concerns a woman who threw herself off the bridge. The incident of the "brusque volte-face" and resounding laughter is first in the diegesis. The last concerns the sighting of a black dot on the sea and the present cry of gulls. All three are siren stories.

There is no reason to suspect that the Dantesque elements before and after the conversion will differ, since the concretion of isotopes seems to take place purely in the language. But one problem has revealed itself--the problem inherent to thematic multiplicity, as any single element of the rewriting is not necessarily limited to suggest a precise circle or even canticle. The resulting loss of barriers is all the more acceptable as Jean-Baptiste expresses his goal to "invert the reasoning." There is no justification for the separation of realms, particularly as duplicity and paradox collapse in a world of duality--the duplicity of lie or the truth of paradox.

Even if it is only the present point of view which confers the resemblance of the present upon the past through the isotopes of the rewriting (the isotopes of the past confirm those of the present and vice versa, just as Camus's previous works are capable of further confirming the isotopes of *La Chute* while *La Chute* concretizes so many of the literal occurrences of these previous works into the isotopes of the Dantesque rewriting), the *récit*'s own coherent structures tell us that Jean-Baptiste is aware that he was living a lie. The rewriting therefore differs from the *récit* in that it reads all the way through what the *récit* only reveals at its end--that is, immobility, circularity, and really no conversion at all. Making the acceptance of the *Inferno* within himself the right direction, Clamence turns the lowest of realms into a mark of salvation and purification. Before the conversion, the "good" life was infernal. The conversion will change nothing other than to accelerate the fall, since, after that decisive moment, Jean-Baptiste accepts duplicity within himself rather than allowing it to exist with respect to the outside. Similarly, Amsterdam is more suited to the role of the *Inferno* than in Paris, even though the latter is also described as an "illusion," inhabited by "shades," and characterized by its "autumn leaves," "rain," "river," circular motion, and more. The new setting of Amsterdam only intensifies what was always there. The resulting immobility is also reflected in the fact that the above elements are frequent ones of Camus's works prior to *La Chute* and that, furthermore, these anterior settings are often capable of further realizing and strengthening the *récit*'s isotopes, thus proving the latter to be a destiny and synthesis.

The extent to which the rewriting functions in the second through sixth divisions of the *récit* is most striking, even if massively suggestive and rewritten passages like those at which the *récit*'s first portion arrive seem to have dissolved in part. Added and gradual specificity now directs our attention.

Let us begin with Paolo and Francesca, who possibly existed in the *récit*'s first portion, in the recurrent juxtaposition of the *lecteurs* and the *fornicateurs*. In the third part of the *récit*, Clamence stresses the error associated with words, movement with no progress, books hardly read in conjunction with possessing women, and finally the movement of others who follow without being able to grasp anything. These elements, in such proximity, certainly allow for the deformation of figurative language to produce the *contrapasso* of Canto V of the *Inferno*.

> J'avançais ainsi à la surface de la vie, dans
> les mots en quelque sorte, jamais dans la
> réalité. Tous ces livres à peine lus, . . .
> ces femmes à peine prises! . . . Les êtres
> suivaient, ils voulaient s'accrocher, mais
> il n'y avait rien, et c'était le malheur.
> (p. 1501)

Let us recall that in Canto V of the *Inferno*, Francesca tells the story of how it was while they were reading the tale of Lancelot and Guinevere's love, that she and Paolo "closed the book" and "read no more," another one of those lines which raises the problem of interpretation:

> 'Quel giorno più non vi legemmo avanti.'
> (*Inferno* V, 138)

As we have already allowed Clamence's words to suggest the punishment in the impossibility to descend from motion, let us recall this precise context of *s'accrocher* as already seen in reference to the gods' flight in descent (p. 1482), a proven pattern of meaning for the whole of the *récit*. It produces an interesting image at the beginning of the fourth division:

> Les colombes attendent là-haut, elles attendent toute l'année. Elles tournent au-dessus de la terre, regardent, voudraient descendre. Mais il n'y a rien, que la mer, les canaux, des toits couverts d'enseignes, et nulle tête où se poser.
> (pp. 1512-1513)

The dove imagery of Paolo and Francesca's Canto V now evokes only too precisely the above words and the imprisonment in the "whirlwind of passion." The above words also root themselves in the marks of the *Inferno* already shown to be a constituent element of Clamence's obsessional world of words, including the ever-present canals, *enseignes*, the insistance on heads, and of course, the sea-going voyage and doomed flight. Another conclusive mark of the Francesca da Rimini episode, within the writing, occurs in the fifth part of the *récit*:

> Je cherchai donc ailleurs l'amour promis par les livres, et que je n'avais jamais rencontré dans la vie.
> (p. 1527)

The above words follow Clamence's expression of the perversion of love, and the present juxtaposition of his search for it to literature suggests the "closing of the book" and the misinterpretation of literature. The juxtaposition of literature and love is a clear and recurrent obsession with Clamence, and, in the next paragraph, the isotope is astoundingly confirmed:

> En tout cas, loin de me trouver transporté et absous dans l'éternité, comme on dit, de la passion, j'ajoutai encore au poids de mes fautes et à mon égarement. J'en conçus une telle horreur de l'amour que, pendant des années, je ne pus entendre sans grincer des dents *la Vie en rose ou la Mort d'amour d'Yseult*.
> (p. 1527)

Clamence conveys again the sense of ceaseless motion in the context of "eternity," "fault," "passion," and courtly literature. But most striking in the above passage is Clamence's consciousness of figurative language to extend its metaphors, to produce a visual world, and the *contrapasso* becomes explicit. Even Clamence stresses the deformation as he interrupts his idiom with: "comme on *dit*." Furthermore, he continues idiomatic expression beyond the "whirlwind of passion" to the "weight" of his "faults," just as the weight of the material world is also a stressed factor of Canto V. The "whirlwind," "error," "eternity," "passion," "love," literature, the refusal of literature, and "death" form a tightly knit anticipated network of elements; and the reference to courtly love is present throughout the *récit* as well as in excessive reminders of Clamence's heroic exploits and *courtoisie* (pp. 1486, 1501, 1519, and 1520).

Of course, the subjects of literature and death also make Brunetto Latini's presence suspect in these same pages. One should keep in mind his circular motion under the rain of fire, his stopping to talk to Dante-pilgrim and Virgil, his guilt in having taught "come l'uomo s'eterna" (*Inferno* XV, 85) through literature, the fact of being Dante's teacher, his punishment in the circle of the sodomites, his guilt in having perverted the nature of language and in having defied death and generation, and the final image of the race he seems to run as he tries to catch up with the next group.

The same passages containing the seeds of Paolo and Francesca's Canto V also give way to a more precise Brunetto Latini, only suggested in the first portion of the récit, in the vague juxtaposition of eternal life, lyricism, circular motion, and teaching, among a multitude of other elements. As the isotope is further realized, Jean-Baptiste will once again assimilate the Dantesque presence to the first person of the récit:

> J'étais comme mes Hollandais qui sont là sans y être. . . . Je n'imaginais l'amour d'Yseult que dans les romans. . . . Je roulais. . . . Malheur à vous quand tous les hommes diront du bien de vous; Ah! Celui-là qui parlait d'or. . . . La machine se mit donc à avoir des arrêts. . . . La pensée de mort fit irruptions. . . . Je mesurais les années qui me séparaient de ma fin. . . . Je cherchais des exemples d'hommes . . . qui fussent déjà morts. . . . Qu'importait le mensonge d'un homme dans l'histoire des générations?
> (pp. 1520-1521)

The above passage clearly interweaves the presences of Paolo and Francesca and Brunetto Latini. Appropriate for both subjects, the misuse of literature is the subject of Clamence's next lines:

> Je cherchais donc ailleurs l'amour promis par
> les livres. . . . Je ne pus entendre *La Vie en
> rose* ou *La Mort d'amour d'Yseult*.
> (p. 1527)

Jean-Baptiste immediately speaks at great length on his desire for immortality in such lines as the following, only one of numerous examples which conform Brunetto's obsession:

> [J]e mourais d'envie d'être immortel.
> (p. 1527)

Let us now digress for a moment to examine the approach to one of the *récit*'s metacritical moments. After his lengthy speech on immortality, Jean-Baptiste refers to his "débauche" (p. 1528) as "une jungle sans avenir ou passé, sans promesse. . . ." With respect to the *Commedia*'s diegesis, this statement is immediately followed by a precise allusion to the inscription on Dante's Gates of Hell:

> On laisse en y entrant la crainte comme l'espérance.
> (p. 1528)

This is almost a direct echo of the inscription:

> Lasciate ogni speranza voi che entrate.
> (*Inferno* III, 9)

La Chute's echo of the above inscription is one of three such references during the course of the *récit*. But, returning to the notion of a gradual concretion on the literal level of the rewriting, one should note that this last reference to the *Inferno* follows immediately the pages on courtly love, literature, death, and immortality, and perhaps permit the reader with more justification to place this discourse clearly within the context of Dante's *Commedia*. Therefore, even though the elements which possibly exist in terms of Paolo and Francesca and Brunetto Latini are not massivley precise, the approach to this metacritical moment may well support their Dantesque interpretation. Let us recall that in the first part of the *récit*, the literal presences of the "last circle" and "concentric circles" in Hell followed a lengthy passage which struck us as densely populated with Dantesque elements. It will be interesting to note whether this sort of continuity is always apparent through proximity.

Let us now examine the full realization of the presence of Pope Nicholas III within the whole of the *récit* and follow Jean-Baptiste's assimilation of the isotope. His presence was only apparent among vague hints of corruption, the "coincé," and the suggestion of fire at the end of the *récit*'s first portion. It is in the second portion that Clamence's words confirm the validity of those first hints in terms of the rewriting. The second occurrence of "coincé" coincides with the near identification of the Dantesque simoniac.

> Si le destin m'avait obligé de choisir un métier
> manuel, tourneur ou couvreur, soyez tranquille,
> j'eusse choisi les toits et fait amitié avec
> les vertiges. Les soutes, les cales, les sou-
> terrains, les grottes, les gouffres, me fai-
> saient horreur. J'avais même voué une haine
> spéciale pour les spéléologues, qui avaient
> le front d'occuper la première page. . . .
> S'efforcer de parvenir à la côte moins huit
> cents, au risque de se trouver la tête coincée
> dans un goulet rocheux (un siphon, comme disent
> ces inconscients!) me paraissait l'exploit de
> caractères pervertis ou traumatisés. Il y avait
> du crime là-dessous.
> (pp. 1487-1488)

The use of the word *coincé* proves productive! Such a precise context in the second of its occurrences would almost suffice for the identification of the Pope, but his isotope will be even further realized. In the above passage, Clamence refers to underground regions and even funnels, recalling precisely the rocky funnels formed in the eighth and ninth circles of Malebolge, realm of Lower Hell and Fraud, which includes, in their configuration, the rocky holes of Canto XIX's parody of San Giovanni's baptismal fonts. Like Dante, Jean-Baptiste also qualifies the people associated wtih such places as being upside down, which confirms further the isotope of Dante's Pope Nicholas. In third place, it becomes a question for Jean-Baptiste of these people having "la tête coincée dans un goulet rocheux." These last words could not be more explicitly those which define Pope Nicholas' situation, stuck head first in the rocky funnel and condemned to be squashed further and further into the rocky crevices as his corrupt successors arrive.

The realization of the above Dantesque presence takes place in a time before Jean-Baptiste's "brusque volte-face" or conversion, and therefore his hate of underground regions and of the people associated with them has no relationship to this assimilation and realization of the isotope. The language accomplishes the task in spite of place, time, and character.

Pope Nicholas III continues to make his presence progressively heard in the following lines:

> Le crime tient sans trêve le devant de la scène,
> mais le criminel n'y figure que fugitivement
> pour être aussitôt remplacé.
> (p. 1489)

Just one page beyond the reference to upside down people in rocky funnels the above words describe precisely the punishment for Pope Nicholas: when Boniface, the successor to Pope Nicholas, dies, he will come to the same spot and push Nicholas further down into the rocky hole.

In the fifth part of the *récit*, the use of "coincé" occurs again (p.1531), and again the literal use of the word evokes the Pope's presence in the following precise reference to the baptismal font and the fact of not being able to get out of it:

> Nous ne sortirons jamais de ce bénitier immense. . . . J'étais toujours coincé.
> (p. 1531)

The rocky hole of Canto XIX is explicitly the parody of a baptismal font, Nicholas just has made a mockery of holy office and now finds himself stuck upside down in it forever. The image is also a reminder of the anecdote given by Dante at the beginning of Canto XIX as he tells of how he saved a drowning victim of San Giovanni by breaking the stone of the font:

> L'un de le quali, ancor non e molt' anni, Rupp'
> io per un che dentro v' annegava;
> (*Inferno* XIX, 19-20)

The isotope continues to realize further its presence in the sixth and final part of the *récit*, and this is the ultimately irrefutable mark in the identification process, as

Jean-Baptiste announces the fact of being elected Pope, and how he used his powers for his own personal gain:

> [J]'étais Pape. . . . [J]'ai été nommé Pape . . .
> (p. 1537)

Even the recurrent "Pope" and his own insistence on the "name" supports our theory of assimilation. Jean-Baptiste's assimilation of isotopes is probably clearest in the example of Pope Nicholas: he passes from the "coincé" which applies to the people of Holland, to the "coincé" and rocky underground funnels which apply to the upside down people he hates, to the collective form of the first person in his reference to all of "us" being stuck in the font, and eventually to himself as having been elected Pope. He reflects and assimilates the isotopic elements in the process of self-accusation and self-purgation designed by and for himself as well as for others, which makes his voyage resemble Dante's pilgrim's insofar as the latter does the same thing as he passes through the circles on an upward path. Regarding Clamence, reflection also becomes more and more a part of the literal level of the *récit*, thematically, as shown above in the assimilation process, but also literally at the end of *La Chute* when Jean-Baptiste will actually address his client as the mirror image of himself.

Clamence's assimilation of the Pope's isotope is what prompts one to look for the same thing in other isotopes. Another example of the assimilation of elements to the first person of the *récit* and in the passage from the thematic to the literal image is found in the thematic role and image of decapitation. It first occurred in the metaphoric sense where the omnipresence of the mouth seemed to stand for the barman (as it stands for Clamence himself all the way through his dramatic monologue), to the people with their heads in the neon clouds, and eventually to Jean-Baptiste in the first person, as he supposes his own decapitation and his head served on a platter.

With such emphasis on hate, immobility, and confinement, the *récit* inevitably continues to confirm the active role of the traitor of Canto XXXIII who ate his children. Clamence's discourses are so overwhelmingly typified by hate, revenge and treachery, that to list all instances of their existence is not possible nor as productive as just making a general note of the pervading atmosphere of the *récit* and point out a few examples. For example, men are transformed into dogs in the "chiens écumants" (p. 1485), and Jean-Baptiste extends the figurative language once again, to say, "Cet homme enrageait littéralement de se trouver dans son tort . . ." (p. 1485). The passage ends in death. This example does point out the concern with literal meaning which is by no means only characteristic of *La Chute*. Within *La Chute*, the disfigurement of language includes mythologization, literal contamination, the passage from the figurative to the literal, and from literal to literal--all marks of the immobilization and inversion that typify the *Inferno* culminating in the last circle with Ugolino's parody of the Word made Flesh.

Ugolino's presence continues to make itself heard in the following lines, as the elements of prison, the tower, and the literal obsession, about to make itself clear, form a narrative and related theoretical and literal sequence of terms:

> Selon moi, on ne méditait pas dans les caves ou les cellules des prisons (à moins qu'elles fussent situées dans une tour, avec une vue étendue); on y moisissait.
> (p. 1488)

The same elements to suggest Ugolino's presence in the first part of the *récit* present themselves again; however, Ugolino's presence does not account for the striking element of "mold," particularly in the above conjunction with "cellars." One is reminded that Dante, in his discussion of the degeneracy of the Fransiscans, compares these people to bad wine molding in the cellar.[2]

Following the reference to "mold," the confirmation of the isotope is strengthened:

> Et je comprenais cet homme qui, étant entré dans les ordres, défroqua, parce que sa cellule, au lieu d'ouvrir, donnait sur un mur. . . .
> Je ne moisissais pas.
> (p. 1488)

Within Camus's text, "mold" has joined the "orders" to produce a further confirmation of the isotope. One also remarks the passage from "on" to "je" which points, once again, to the assimilation on the part of Jean-Baptiste. While the immobilization factor and the presence of the cell are approaching a decisive moment of the *récit*, the immobilization to be assimilated by Jean-Baptiste, the Franciscan's isotope is about to emerge once and for all with the final word of the following passage:

> Vos voisins ont besoin de tragédie, que voulez-vous, c'est leur petite transcendance, c'est leur apéritif. D'ailleurs, est-ce un hasard si je vous parle de concierge? J'en avais un, vraiment disgracié, la méchanceté même, un monstre d'insignifiance et de rancune, qui aurait découragé un franciscain.
> (pp. 1492-1493)

Let us return specifically to the underlying presence of Ugolino as Jean-Baptiste discourses at length on slavery, obligation, and even dwells upon the literal extension of "flesh" and the literal consciousness of words in the passage to follow the one cited above concerning men and dogs, and precisely literal rage:

> En particulier, la chair, la matière, le physique en un mot, qui déconcerte ou décourage tant d'hommes dans l'amour ou dans la solitude, m'apportait, sans m'asservir, des joies égales. J'étais fait pour avoir un corps.
> (p. 1490)

The sum of bondage, the flesh, a concern with words, love, and servitude, all points to the presence of Ugolino. The terms of the context continue to include friendship and the prison cell:

> Un homme dont l'ami avait été emprisonné . . . couchait tous les soirs sur le sol de sa chambre. . . .
> (p. 1490)

The above situation evokes precisely that of Ugolino and Ruggieri in the perversion of their bond, once friendship: the traitor placed the other traitor in the Tower of Hunger to starve to death and sealed him in the room forever. The reader would do well to keep in mind that it will soon be Jean-Baptiste who is lying down, locked in a room, and about to die as the process of assimilation reveals itself to be valid in yet another case.

Ugolino continues to be an active presence:

> C'est le mort frais que nous aimons chez nos amis, le mort douloureux, notre émotion, nous-mêmes enfin.
> (p. 1497)

The same passage stresses the mouth and eating:

> Comme nous aimons les amis qui viennent de nous quitter, n'est-ce pas? Comme nous admirons ceux de nos maîtres qui ne parlent plus, la bouche pleine de terre.
> (p. 1497)

This presence of the "mouth" has already revealed itself, particularly in reference to the "host" of the opening passages of the *récit*. Also, one must not forget the fact that Ugolino's Canto XXXIII of the *Inferno* includes the Treacherous Hosts whose presence is illustrated by the story of a poisoning at the dinner table, as Frate Alberigo had two of his family members murdered. While Clamence's above words evoke more clearly Ugolino through the presence of a chewing mouth and the loss of a friend, the use of "maîtres" and the "mouth," in the company of the breaking of bonds, could support the identification of Treacherous Hosts. Canto XXXIII's Treacherous Hosts are soon to make their presence known:

> J'ai toujours voulu être servi avec le sourire. Si la bonne avait l'air triste, elle empoisonnait mes journées. . . . Mais je me disais qu'il valait mieux pour elle qu'elle fît son service en riant plutôt qu'en pleurant. . . . De la même manière, je refusais toujours de manger

> dans les restaurants chinois. Pourquoi? Parce que les Asiatiques, lorsqu'ils se taisent, et devant les Blancs, ont souvent l'air méprisant. Comment jouir alors du poulet laqué, comment surtout, en les regardant, penser qu'on a raison?
>
> (p. 1499)

While the above use of "empoisonnait" is figurative, the context allows for the deformation. The literal presence of tears is also a mark of Canto XXXIII, as these sinners are characterized by their inability to cry. The "air méprisant" is a typical mark of Clamence's discourse, and strengthens the relationship of this passage to the initial one of the text. Along with the stress on servitude and eating, the above elements suggest the underlying presence of the Treacherous Hosts. The next paragraph includes servitude, sitting down at the table, and the famous *enseignes*, and culminates, once again, in the explicit reference to Hell and classification. One undoubtedly concludes the presence of the Treacherous Hosts and Ugolino in the preceding pages, especially as the process of gradual concretion was seen to function so clearly in the last paragraphs of the *récit*'s first portion, where the *enseignes* and so many other elements lead to the identification of the last circle of Hell. The Treacherous Host's isotope emerges so clearly:

> Tout à fait entre nous, la servitude, souriante de préférence, est donc inévitable. Mais nous ne devons pas le reconnaître. Celui qui ne peut s'empêcher d'avoir des esclaves, ne vaut-il pas mieux qu'il les appelle hommes libres? . . . Aussi, pas d'enseignes, et celle-ci est scandaleuse. D'ailleurs, si tout le monde se mettait à table, hein, affichait son vrai métier, son identité, on ne saurait plus où donnait la tête!

> Imaginez des cartes de visite: Dupont, philo-
> sophe froussard, ou propriétaire chrétien, ou
> humaniste adultère, on a le choix, vraiment.
> Mais ce serait l'enfer! Oui, l'enfer doit être
> ainsi: des rues à enseignes et pas moyen de
> s'expliquer. On est classé une fois pour
> toutes.
> (p. 1499)

The obsession with classification and the *enseignes* is definitely a sign of Hell as seen in regard to the alst pages of the first part of the text and continues to function afterwards on a massive scale. If the idea of a gradual concretion is to function, the above passage is almost metacritical and should give one the right to conclude that the rewriting was at work in preceding passages of the account. The synecdochical "mouth" or "head" also plays an evident role in the gradual concretion of the isotopes, culminating in the final decapitation. Similarly, the *Inferno* insists upon the "mouth" and gradually the "mouth" becomes more and more of literal importance, as one nears Ugolino, the Hosts, and Lucifer chewing the three traitors at the center of the Earth.

Another word which incites suspicion of the Dantesque presence is the use of literal "sticking" in the use of *collé*, which brings us, once again, back to the presence of Ugolino and Ruggieri in Canto XXXIII, as the two characters are literally attached to each other in the chewing process and in the immobility of the ice. Clamence refers to a woman who "s'est collée . . . avec un faraud . . ." (p. 1494), and he will succeed, as usual, in assimilating the isotope:

> Je finis par m'attacher à elle comme j'imagine
> que le geôlier se lie à son prisonnier.
> (p. 1508)

Jean-Baptiste's obsessional *liens, lier, coller (se), s'attacher*--
all are marks of his language throughout the work and evoke the
existing Dantesque relationship between Ugolino and Ruggieri.
Clamence's above words bring the relationship between jailor
and prisoner to the deformed literal level of our reading.
The fifth division of the *récit* provides further confirmation
of this Dantesque presence, in the astounding juxtaposition
of the "prison cell," immobilization of the body up to the
level of the neck, the action of "wiping," and "closing ones
eyes." It is interesting to note that Clamence specifies that
this all stems from an invention of the Middle Ages in a
lengthy description of the "immuable contrainte qui ankylosait
son corps," which includes a discussion of the "innocent prisoner." These elements surely announce the anticipated isotope,
as, most often, Ugolino is viewed as a tragic victim of circumstances.

> La solide porte . . . s'arrête à la hauteur du menton.
> (p. 1532)

The isotope takes shape. While "cells" occupy a large part
of the *récit*, and particularly as Jean-Baptiste has identified
the cell as an invention of mankind during the Middle Ages
(p. 1531), the following lines are exemplary in their juxtaposition of rewritten elements.

> Le prisonnier, coincé dans la cellule, ne peut
> s'essuyer, bien qu'il lui soit permis, il est
> vrai, de fermer les yeux. . . . [C]'est une
> invention d'hommes.
> (p. 1532)

The action of "wiping" is one of the initial elements of Ugolino's Canto XXXIII. Besides, the action of closing ones eyes is of major literal concern in the lines regarding the Treacherous Hosts of Canto XXXIII: as they try to cry, the tears freeze their eyes shut, and the description is a lengthy one:

> Lo pianto stesso li pianger non lascia,
> E 'l duol, che trova in su li occhi rintoppo,
> Si volge in entre a far crescer l' ambascia;
> Che le lagrime prime fanno groppo,
> E, si come visiere di cristallo,
> Riempion sotto 'l ciglio tutto il coppo.
> (*Inferno* XXXIII, 94-99)

In the first lines of Canto XXXIII, the "mouth," the "feast," the "chewing" at the "nape of the neck," "wiping" the mouth before speaking, the immobilization in the ice, and position of the two heads overtake the account by virtue of their initial placement:

> La bocca sollevò dal fiero pasto
> Quel peccator, forbendola a' capelli
> Del capo ch' elli avea di retro guasto
> Poi cominciò; 'Tu vuo' chi' io rinnovelli
> Disperato dolor che 'l cor mi preme . . .
> (*Inferno*, XXXIII, 1-5)

Several isotopes of Clamence's monologue interweave themselves in the literal presences of food and confinement, but the "tears," the "wiping," and the "nape of the neck," are signs of Canto XXXIII; ultimately the attachment of the jailor to his prisoner marks Ugolino's presence and confirms the other elements as such. Ugolino's presence is then further confirmed in the specificity of being locked in a room, as Clamence insists on the process:

> Avez-vous bien fermé la porte?
> (p. 1541)

These words do not initially strike one as meaningful, but the insistance which follows succeeds in deforming the language. We are lead, once again, to concretize the isotope, which includes the fact of Ugolino being locked in the Tower of Hunger to starve to death, when Clamence speaks the following words:

> J'ai le complexe du verrou. . . . [J]e ne puis jamais savoir si j'ai poussé le verrou. Chaque soir je dois me lever pour le vérifier.
> (p. 1541)

Nails at the door are a pronounced element of Ugolino's *récit*. Clamence also dwells abnormally on the parallel image. His habitual assimilation results in taking care of the barricade from the inside of his room; thus, his immobilization and isolation are carried one step further.

As Jean-Baptiste then assimilates the action of going to bed, he is incapable of tears:

> Je me recouche . . . [J]e ne pleure pas pourtant.
> (p. 1550)

Although not quite as defined as those which occur in reference to the Treacherous Hosts, the inability to cry and the literal presence of tears also play marked roles within Ugolino's own words:

> Io non piangea; sì dentro impetrai:
> Piangevan elli: ed Anselmuccio mio
> Disse: 'Tu guardi sì, padre! Che hai?'
> Perciò non lacrimai, nè rispuos'io . . .
> (*Inferno* XXXIII, 49-52)

[Ugolino's children offer him their flesh,[3] and sacrificed children play a role throughout Jean-Baptiste's *récit* but such examples as "les enfants de la Judée massacrés" (p. 1533) and "Rachel, gémissant sur ses petits enfants tués pour lui" (p. 1533) are too far removed in context for one to include their existence as proof of the rewriting.]

Through the above examples, it becomes evident that Ugolino functions to engender a large part of the *récit*, even though the idea of a gradual concretion is perhaps less suited to his isotope (except in the sense of a cumulative concretion) than the ones already proposed; however, specificity does function to support the validity of the rewriting.

Before discussing the extensive presence of Ulysses in the second through sixth and final parts of the *récit*, we should remind ourselves that Ulysses, as the hero of an anti-voyage, tends to encompass many portions of *La Chute*, directly and indirectly, just as in the *Commedia*.

Ulysses and Cocytus emerged as the rewriting's most defined and irrefutable isotopes, as they followed so systematically a process of gradual concretion into those final and massively rewritten lines of the *récit*'s first part. By contrast, the second part seems to have lost its affiliation with the Dantesque presence; but a closer look at its first lines succeeds in contriving Ulysses' presence as Jean-Baptiste refers to the effects of his words upon his clients as a "tempête" (p. 1484). This language is followed by a reference to his "persuasion et la chaleur" (p. 1484). The storm created by Dante to bring Ulysses to his death, his persuasion, and his tongue of fire are all evoked clearly in this vocabulary. Clamence then adds his "attitude noble" and a high frequency of *mépris*, already shown to typify Clamence's barman as well as several characters of the *Inferno*. While the first part of the *récit* made reference to the flight of gods, Jean-Baptiste's own mythological flight is suggested in the deformation of the following words:

> [J]e ne me suis jamais abaissé non plus à aucune démarche. . . . [J]'ai toujours aimé renseigner les passants dans la rue, leur donner du feu, prêter la main aux charrettes trop lourdes. . . .
> (pp. 1485-1486)

This language obviously makes sense on the earthbound level of the text's own coherence, but unnaturally insists upon altitude, the position of the speaker with respect to humans, and light. The repetition and increasing density permit these elements to acquire explicitly their mythological and heroic meaning, even within the *récit* itself. Jean-Baptiste will literally fly during this account of his past life in Paris, before he went to Amsterdam. The diegesis follows the assimilation of the "mad flight" of gods at the end of the *récit*'s first part. Once again, there is proof that the isotopes occur partly in the language of Clamence's account. In the second part, he continues to assimilate the disdain of the vulgar, the voyage, the heroism, the altitude, the light, and denial of the human world--all leading to the mythological:

> Parlons plutôt de ma courtoisie. Elle était célèbre et pourtant indiscutable. La politesse me donnait en effet de grandes joies. Si j'avais la chance, certains matins, de céder ma place, dans l'autobus ou le métro, à qui le méritait visiblement, de ramasser quelque objet qu'une vieille dame avait laissé tomber et de

> le lui rendre avec un sourire que je connais-
> sais bien, ou simplement de céder mon taxi à
> une personne plus pressée que moi, ma journée
> en était éclairée. Je me réjouissais même,
> il faut bien le dire, de ces jours où, les
> transports publics étant en grêve, j'avais l'oc-
> casion d'embarquer dans ma voiture, aux points
> d'arrêts des autobus, quelques-uns de mes mal-
> heureux concitoyens, empêchés de rentrer chez
> eux. Quitter enfin mon fauteuil, au théâtre,
> pour permettre à un couple d'être réuni, placer
> en voyage les valises d'une jeune fille dans
> le filet placé trop haut pour elle, étaient
> autant d'exploits que j'accomplissais plus sou-
> vent que d'autres parce que j'étais plus atten-
> tif aux occasions de le faire et que j'en re-
> tirais des plaisirs mieux savourés.
> (pp. 1486-1487)

The confirmation of those elements which continue to identify Ulysses' presence are seen below, as the "vulgar" is named in opposition to Clamence's own attained height, and as human "virtue" comes into play as sufficing in itself:

> [C]'est atteindre plus haut que l'ambitieux
> vulgaire et se hisser à ce point culminant où
> le vertu ne se nourrit plus que d'elle-même.
> (p. 1497)

Ulysses is literally present above: Dante makes him guilty of ignoring divine guidance in his persuasion:

> 'Fatti non foste a viver come bruti,
> Ma per seguir virtute e canoscenza.'
> (*Inferno* XXVI, 119-120)

These are famed lines of the canto, as virtue and knowledge and science do not suffice in Dante's thesis, a correction of the thesis of the *Convivio* and of natural Boethian philosophy. The frequent use of *vertu* in Camus's text, and the above question of "vertu" sufficing in itself is a direct echo of Canto XXVI, including the heroic tone's masking of Ulysses' error in persuading his men to join in the "mad flight" directly towards the island-mount of Purgatory. Clamence's words also break with humanity. Altitude and light take on a new concretized meaning as they approach Clamence's "summit;" likewise for "giving someone a light" and "lending someone a hand" which make idiomatic sense without the mythological or symbolic intervention; however, the excessive instance on altitude, light, and heroic language points to the mythologization of words. Their repetition clearly removes them from their every day usage. The deformation proves valid, as a voyage to the sun, Elijah's, is in the making, and Jean-Baptiste will say:

> Je suis . . . Elie sans messie. . . .
> (p. 1535)

The simile of Elijah's voyage in the Ulysses episode is ironic, since it is a successful one, willed by God. Jean-Baptiste Clamence's usual assimilation of the isotope reinforces an awareness of the lie and duplicity; his lucidity in lie, at least verbally, turns duplicity into a mark of salvation.

The altitude is literally confirmed in the following passage where it takes on its physical and geographical weight of meaning, similar to the previously discerned concretion of the *coeur*. The figurative passes to the literal. Jean-Baptiste even stresses that his listener will find "l'expression exacte en ce qui [le] concerne" (p. 1485):

> Arrêtons-nous sur ces cimes. Vous comprenez
> maintenant ce que je voulais dire en parlant
> de viser plus haut. Je parlais justement de
> ces points culminants, les seuls où je puisse

> vivre. Oui je ne me suis jamais senti à l'aise
> que dans les situations élevées. Jusque dans
> le détail de la vie, j'avais besoin d'être au-
> dessus. Je préférais l'autobus au métro, les
> calèches aux taxis, les terrasses aux entresols.
> Amateur des avions de sports, où l'on porte
> la tête en plein ciel, je figurais aussi, sur
> les bateaux l'éternel promeneur des dunet-
> tes. . . .
>
> (pp. 1487)

The above passage continues to encompass those elements which realized to such a large extent the presence of Pope Nicholas III in the people of underground regions and the rocky funnels. In the above passage, the physical characteristic of elevation has successfully deformed figurative and poetic meaning to engender a good portion of the text, but again we are faced with the problem of multiplicity: with respect to Dante's Ulysses, the summit reached could either be the true summit of the Earthly Paradise or the summit of Ulysses' presumption--that is, the summit of the island upon whose shore Ulysses shipwrecks, or the summit to which Dante-pilgrim is not premitted to acceed directly. The ambiguity was also apparent at the end of the first part of the *récit* regarding the return to the last circle from the shore of either Canto I of the *Inferno* or Canto I of the *Purgatorio*. Likewise, the present image of "la tête en plein ciel" echoes the image created at the end of the first part of the *récit*; assimilated now by Jean-Baptiste, it once applied to the people of Holland with their heads in the clouds of metallic light, in pointing to the possible suggestion of Ulysses' punishment in the double tongue of fire, the souls of the Vestibule with their "testa cinta," or even Justinian. One must again be aware of the fact that the image of the first part of the *récit* took place in a time following the presently discussed image of figurative decapitation. Once again, there is proof that the progress of the *récit*, and not real time, provides for the realization of the isotopes. The time of the *récit* supports the thesis that the fall was ever-present; the *récit*, particularly as a rewriting, announces all the way through what the account's existence with respect to real time only announces at its brief references to time after the conversion: the rewriting announces the fall within Paris and therefore within the majority of the text, since most of the *récit* is devoted to this former period in time, a period of realization. Like Dante's Ulysses, Jean-Baptiste's heroic account of a flight is ironic, as it is actually the story of a fall. While Jean-Baptiste's breaking of bonds with humanity is all too well suggested in the expression of having reached the summit, far from the "vulgar," and the infinite and the shore of the "éternel promeneur des dunettes," he insists on having broken his bonds with humanity in this next passage:

> Un balcon naturel, à cinq ou six cents mètres
> au-dessus d'une mer encore visible et baignée
> de lumière était au contraire l'endroit où je
> respirais le mieux, surtout si j'étais seul,
> bien au-dessus des fourmis humaines.
> (p. 1488)

The rewriting practically forces one to imagine the summit of the Earthly Paradise to which Ulysses' presumption allows him to aspire. The island, the light, the solitude, and the breaking of bonds with humanity--all are elements which continue to confirm the underlying presence of Dante's anti-hero. Even the Earthly Paradise is very soon to surface literally. "Fire" will also return to the heroic and mythological level as Clamence remarks, "[L]es miracles de feu se fissent sur des hauteurs accessibles."

At that supposed point of elevation and perfection in his life, Jean-Baptiste describes the unity achieved in terms which could apply so well to what the end of the *Paradiso* strives for; "la vie en prise directe" in a "lumière édénique" (p. 1489), and his perfect "accord avec la vie" (p. 1489), which goes so far as to include his knowledge of everything at birth, again suggesting the *canoscenza* of Ulysses' presumption. Such unity implies the correction of division from the self (the Augustinian *obblio*), to which Clamence alludes os often, all the while describing unity, even though the ironic distance drags it all down into the "error" or wandering off the straight path of the *Inferno* (most precisely in Ulysses' canto). Furthermore, the division from self proves to be an element of Camus's previous works. One conclusive instance of its occurrence is found in "Pluies de New York" which literally revolves around elements of rain, exile, loss of hope, a slope, shades, islands, cries, infernal noises, madness, tears, hate, the sea, a song which calls out to the passerby, burning, lights, creatures, flesh, the center, and culminating in the final sentence which defines the place as "un lieu de délivrance où l'on pourra . . . se perdre enfin sans jamais se retrouver."

Hell, the Augustinian sin, and salvation find themselves in the company of one another, just as they do within *La Chute*. While the rewriting is not concretized as in the latter, it is retrospectively present and contains a relatively high density of elements suitable to the Dantesque rewriting; but it cannot be considered as such in its own unity due to the lack of an anticipatory phenomenon, of specificity, and of gradual concretion of isotopes.

Jean-Baptiste reveals an obsession with memory and loss of it, a broad category of language with respect to the *Commedia*. It is a common trait for the sinners of the first canticle to ask to be remembered on Earth, but it is also in the Earthly Paradise that the role of the river,[4] Lethe, permits loss of memory to the pilgrim. Within the context of *La Chute*, Clamence associates more than once rivers, loss of memory, and blood: for example, he tells the tale of a man who brought on his daughter's suicide and subsequently "retournait à la rivière pour oublier, disait-il. Le calcul était juste, il oublia" (p. 1513). "Suicide" and "memory" (or lack of it) pervade. In Dante's configuration, from the Wood of the Suicides to the plain under the rain of fire, the river of boiling blood must be crossed. Even Dante-pilgrim juxtaposes the two rivers as he leaves the Wood and Virgil answers his question:

> . . . 'Maestro, ove si trova
> Flegetonta e Lete? Chè dell'un taci,
> E l' altro di che si fa d' esta piova?'
> 'In tutte tue question certo mi piaci'
> Rispuose; 'ma 'l bollor dell'acqua rossa
> Dovea ben solver l'une che tu faci.

> Letè vedrai, ma fuor di questa fossa,
> Là dove vanno l'anime a lavarsi
> Quando la colpa pentuta è rimossa.'
>
> (*Inferno* XIV, 130-138)

La Chute's two suicide accounts (or three if we include Clamence's final plunge) verbally occur in conjunction with rivers. The images of Clamence's language and, with some respect for the diegesis of the *Commedia*, continue to form an overlay to the river of Dante's Earthly Paradise where loss of memory plays a constituent role. As Jean-Baptiste's memory recovers the remembrance of the incident at the source of the obsessional "laughter" in conjunction with crossing the bridge over the river, the high frequency of "laughter" and "loss of memory" is not surprising.

The first in the diegesis of the three siren stories, or second in terms of historical time, is preceded by the following figurative and literal flight in Jean-Baptiste's approaching recovery of the memory of the original incident:

> [E]lle m'a soulevé longtemps au-dessus du train quotidien et j'ai plané littéralement, pendant des années. . . . J'ai plané jusqu'au soir où... Mais non, ceci est une autre affaire et il faut l'oublier. . . . J'allais de fête en fête. Il m'arrivait de danser pendant des nuits, de plus en plus fou des êtres et de la vie. . . . Je courais ainsi, toujours comblé, jamais rassasié, sans savoir où m'arrêter . . . jusqu'au soir . . . où la musique s'est arrêtée, les lumières se sont éteintes. . . . Mais permettez-moi de faire appel à notre ami le primate. Hochez la tête . . . et surtout buvez avec moi. . . .
>
> (pp. 1490-1491)

A backwards movement is once again traced with respect to the *Commedia*: it passes from having reached an altitude, to the lack of boundaries, to the literal terms of madness, song, loss of light, the night, the gorilla, and finally to the synecdochical head and the use of *hocher*. The last three elements in this series take us back to the very first paragraph of the *récit*. The majority of the passage, as suggested through the above selected literal elements, traces the fall of Ulysses--the same fall traced through alternate elements of his antivoyage's flight as discerned at the end of the first part of *récit* to include the plural evocation of the shore of Dante-pilgrim's arrival in the "dark wood," the shore of the island of Purgatory, and the return to the "last circle," if the "conversion" were successful--that is, unsuccessful. Similarly, the passage cited above thematically echoes Jean-Baptiste's ironic survival of the shipwreck to apparently proceed in Dante-pilgrim's path.

Jean-Baptiste's account of that decisive incident of "laughter" traces again the same backwards route and parallels even more precisely the entrapment of the souls at the end of the first division of the *récit*, foreseen in its flight of gods trying to descend and the "islands where men die insane and happy."

The following passage uses again those literal terms of islands, elevation, boats, night, and other elements which succeed in evoking the fallen direction of Dante's Ulysses' course:

> Je ne m'ennuyais pas puisque je régnais. Le soir dont je vous parle, je peux même dire que je m'ennuyais moins que jamais. Non, vraiment, je ne désirais pas que quelque chose arrivât.

> Et pourtant... Voyez-vous, cher monsieur,
> c'était un beau soir d'automne, encore tiède
> sur la ville, déjà humide sur Seine. La nuit
> venait, les lampadaires brillaient faiblement.
> Je remontais, les quais de la rive gauche vers
> la pont des Arts. On voyait luire le fleuve,
> entre les boîtes fermées des bouquinistes.
> Il y avait peu de monde sur les quais; Paris
> mangeait déjà. Je foulais les feuilles jaunes
> et poussiéreuses qui rappelaient encore l'été.
> Le ciel se remplissait peu à peu d'étoiles qu'on
> apercevait fugitivement en s'éloignant d'un
> lampadaire vers un autre. Je goûtais le silence
> revenu, la douceur du soir, Paris vide. J'étais
> content. La journée avait été bonne; un aveugle,
> la réduction de peine que j'espérais, la chaude
> poignée de main de mon client, quelques générosités et, dans l'après-midi une brillante improvisation, devant quelques amis, sur la dureté du coeur de notre classe dirigeante et l'hypocrisie de nos élites.
>
> (pp. 1494-1495)

"Autumn leaves" (or "pages"), loss of light, "shores," "happiness," excessive references to light evoking a flight, "stars," "blindness," "silence," "taste," "hypocrisy," "class," the "sentence" of a pronounced condemnation, and the "dureté du coeur"--all convey once again the engulfment by the last circle and the backwards movement from the shore of the *Purgatorio* and conversion of which "stars" are a sign among others: "le silence revenu" immediately follows the "fugitively perceived stars." The rewritten meaning is strengthened through the insistance on the "peine," the "dureté du coeur," the "classe," and the "hypocrisie," as well as the tracing of Ulysses' false flight and false arrival at the Mount of Purgatory. A point of conversion is foreshadowed in the fact of something happening without Clamence's awareness, during a climb and flight

whose lie is revealed by the reading of the rewriting. The
paradox is confirmed in the next paragraph:

> J'étais monté sur le pont des Arts, désert . . .
> pour regarder le fleuve . . . dans la nuit. . . .
> Face au Vert-Galant, je dominais l'île. Je
> sentais monter en moi un vaste sentiment de
> puissance et . . . d'achèvement, qui dilatait
> mon coeur. Je me redressais et j'allais allumer une cigarette . . . quand . . . un rire
> éclata derrière moi. Surpris, je fis une
> brusque volte-face; il n'y avait personne.
> J'allais jusqu'au garde-fou; aucune péniche,
> aucune barque. Je me retournai vers l'île,
> j'entendis le rire dans mon dos, un peu plus
> lointain, comme s'il descendait le fleuve.
> Je restais là, immobile. . . . Je me rendis
> dans la salle de bains, pour boire un verre
> d'eau. Mon image souriait dans la glace, mais
> il me sembla que mon sourire était double...
> (p. 1495)

Just as Amsterdam's souls, having sighted no boats, turn back from the desert shore to the last circle, to Clamence, to Mexico-City, and to the *genièvre*, these same elements are present in the above account of a previous time when Clamence, as he tells it, absorbs the elements within himself: he turns back, he has no sight of boats, he has a drink, and he is double: Similarly, he is now at an altitude through the literal elements of his climbing and his domination, like the "dieux qui errent au-dessus de nous" in the context of a seagoing voyage, sirens, a call over the water, the breaking of bonds with humanity and madness; a pattern of meaning is provided for the whole of *La Chute*. The fact that the discourse returns to Amsterdam as the scene after a long series of digressions and continues to mark a process of thematic continuity, isotopic formation, and assimilation proves the immobility: as the initial part of the *récit* portrays the present, the isotopes are kept for the most part away from Clamence. As they eventually fall upon him in the subsequent accounts of the past and finally present, the time of the *récit* proves the innability to escape. In the above cited passage, through the evidence supporting the presumption of Ulysses' lie, or the reinforced split between meaning, direction, and word, and inversion depicts itself here in a time before the coherence of Clamence's own *récit* states the undertaking to invert the sins of error. After numerous references to the processes of this goal, Clamence will realize the split as illustrated by the following:

> Pourquoi je n'ai pas restitué le panneau? Ah!
> ah! Vous avez le réflexe policier, vous! . . .
> Enfin, parce que de cette façon, nous sommes
> dans l'ordre. La justice étant définitivement
> séparée de l'innocence, celle-ci sur la croix,
> celle-là au placard, j'ai le champ libre pour
> travailler selon mes convictions.
> (p. 1542)

Jean-Baptiste does however tell us at this point that the laughter put the "order back into things," and that "order" is clearly an inverted direction.

This episode is the conversion point for the Clamence's own story, marking the beginning of the straight path downward and the inward acceptance of duplicity. Even alone, it reveals the post-conversion's corrected or inverted state as a lie whose paradox cannot be sustained and ends in suicide. Likewise, it goes without saying that the assimilations and repetition of textual elements to provide thematic continuity

and a relationship of immobility between past and present--
past and present with respect to the conversion, exist within
La Chute un-rewritten: even the account betrays itself to some
degree as its own textual echoes deny change--that is, until
the final failure, proving again the undertaking to be a lie.
Strengthening the ever-present *déjouement*, inversion, and immobility, the rewriting further realizes the structures that
point to these conclusions; in the formation of isotopes with
no respect to time; in the assimilation of isotopes by Jean-
Baptiste to the first person of the *récit*; in the realization
of the *contrapasso* over the possible identities revealed through
the Dantesque sequences of the rewriting; in the fact that the
most striking isotopic specificity usually occurs in time before the conversion and therefore contrary to the text's cur-
rently situated metacritical moments; in the delineation of
a backwards movement in which the *Purgatorio* is refused--a backwards movement with respect most precisely to the first episode concerning the "last circle," the loss of shore, the
error and the return to Mexico-City--all pointing to the backwards course of the text's own coherence and leading to the
thematic continuity and echoes most precisely discerned
through the rewriting; in the lie and the false flight which
come to exist with respect to Dante's invented Ulysses; and
in the continued coexistence of paradox, lyricism, and infernal presences to arrive at the final unsustainable moment
of miracles and revelation, including the *sauver* and the *lyre*
of his final words, before plunging literally into the water.

Just as Dante's Ulysses remains of continuing thematic importance from beginning to end of the *Commedia*, it should be no surprise that the historically original siren incident will recover the memory of a female figure over the bridge, her cry as heard descending the river, and her body which "s'abat sur l'eau." These elements repeat those seen above as well as the "corps" of the last lines of the first part of the *récit* at the moment of the "last circle"'s synthesis. Likewise, the use of *s'abattre* suggests the movement of bird's wings, especially as Jean-Baptiste uses the same language to describe the movement of doves by where they "battent les ailes." (The very same language is also used by Camus elsewhere in his writings, in reference to birds.) The parallel between the woman who throws herself off the bridge and the descending bird imagery supports further the concrete relationship between Clamence's lady and the siren particularly as Clamence's "doves" echo the incident throughout *La Chute*. One also recalls the first lines of Canto XXVI:

> Che per mare e per terra batti l' ali
> E per lo 'inferno tuo nome si spande.
> *(Inferno* XXVI, 2-3)

At the end of the *récit*'s passage last cited above, Clamence states almost explicitly the simultaneous presence of the duplicity of the *Inferno* and the reflection of the *Paradiso*. The resulting duality is logical, particularly as "laughter" plays a most frequent role in Canto XXVII of the *Purgatorio*'s forest of the Earthly Paradise. Matilda suddenly appears standing between the waters of Eunoe and Lethe, between the waters of the memory of good deeds and the waters which allow one to forget past wrong doings. Laughing Matilda announces her presence as follows:

> Una donna soletta, che si gia
>   Cantando . . . .
> . . . .
>   Ella ridea dall'altra riva.
>   (*Purgatorio* XXVIII, 40-67)

Dante-pilgrim soon earns the right to these waters, and laughter and song continue to appear throughout the canto.

The summit of the Earthly Paradise, the laughter, the woman, the islands and the garden of Clamence's Vert-Galant, the river, the high frequency of forgetfulness and memory in Camus's text--all are constituent elements that make the incident of the *Purgatorio* a suspiciously underlying presence, even though all such marks of salvation with respect to the *Commedia* find themselves irreversibly contaminated or, perhaps more accurately, find themselves cleansed with respect to Clamence's inverse reasoning. *Oubli* plays an obsessively dominant role in the pages to follow. Even the account of that night ends with a reference to drinking water in the context of a conversion point for Clamence's life. This leads to the identification of Dante-pilgrim's right to the waters of Lethe at the end of the *Purgatorio*, in the Earthly Paradise; however, Jean-Baptiste's road to salvation always reveals an acceptance of error, which allows for the betrayal of Matilda and her laughter, turned into siren and song. As Jean-Baptiste's memory slowly arrives at the original siren incident, he remembers:

> Je tremblais je crois de froid et de saisisse-
> ment. J'écoutais toujours immobile.
> (p. 1511)

The language evokes once again the cold and immobility of the last circle of the *Inferno* and reveals them once again as the directing factors of the discourse and signal the fall from all directions.

Jean-Baptiste also describes the form of the woman as "penchée" and of which he only saw "une nuque fraîche et mouil-lée" (p. 1511). The juxtaposition of the bent over form and the nape of the neck are direct echoes of Ugolino's canto. The image is also present in *L'Etranger*, but *La Chute* adds "La tête courbée" (p. 1545), to the rewriting's sequence, which goes once again to prove the infernally isotopic destiny of the *récit*.

The third poem and final of the three siren stories of Camus's *récit* still stems from his memory but concludes with the generalization and Clamence's present point of view in Amsterdam. With the latter, the time of the *récit* and the time of history finally coincide in this last tale in which the judge-penitent, aboard ship, generalizes to the present and to the future the story of the black dot once sighted over the ocean. It was an object which frightened him and from which he tried to turn away; it strengthens the Dantesque function of the two preceding stories, as well as the final failure. The recalled incident, leading to the generalization, is as follows:

> Un jour pourtant, au cours d'un voyage que j'offris à une amie sans lui dire que je le faisais pour fêter ma guérison, je me trouvais à bord d'un transatlantique, sur le pont supérieur, naturellement. Soudain, j'aperçus au large un point noir sur l'océan couleur de fer. Je détournai les yeux aussitôt, mon cœur se mit à battre. Quand je me forçai à regarder, le point noir avait disparu. J'allais crier, appeler stupidement à l'aide, quand je le revis. Il s'agissait d'un de ces débris que les navires laissent derrière eux. Pourtant, je n'avais pu supporter de le regarder, j'avais tout de suite pensé à un noyé. Je compris alors, sans révolte, comme on se résigne à une idée dont on connaît depuis longtemps la vérité, que ce cri qui, des années auparavant, avait retenti sur la Seine, derrière moi, n'avait pas cessé, porté par le fleuve vers les eaux de la Manche, de cheminer dans le monde, à travers l'étendu illimitée de l'océan, et qu'il m'y avait attendu jusqu'à ce jour où je l'avais rencontré. Je compris aussi qu'il continuerait de m'attendre sur les mers et les fleuves, partout enfin où se trouverait l'eau amère de mon baptême. Ici encore, dites-moi, ne sommes-nous pas sur l'eau? Sur l'eau plate, monotone, interminable, qui confond ses limites à celles de la terre? Comment croire que nous allons arriver à Amsterdam? Nous ne sortirons jamais de ce bénitier immense. Ecoutez! N'entendez-vous pas les cris de goélands invisibles? S'ils crient vers nous, à quoi donc nous appellent-ils?
> (pp. 1530-1531)

The last of the siren incidents confirms all suspicions concerning the two preceding ones. The sense of the infinite, the loss of the shore, the immobility, the oceans, the rivers, the turning around, the drowning, the altitude and the seagoing voyage, the cry, the *cœur*, even the use of *retentir* (repeated in the very last passage of the *récit* and one of the first elements of Ulysses' Canto XXVI), the lady and birds, and the baptism--all are structurally of utmost importance in the *récit* and, for the most part, indicative of the Ulysses canto. Even the "truth," which is a recurrent element of the *récit* is a mark of Homer's Ulysses which signals the "parole feinte."[5] Also, the Gorgon and Pope Nicholas III are overwhelmingly present in the above paragraph: this passage is one of the most densely conclusive ones regarding the rewriting and supports the notion of a gradual concretion, as many of the Dantesque narratives interweave themselves, as the cry lures Clamence to digress, as he turns his eyes away, and as he pigeonholes himself in the immense baptismal font. He already has assimilated the "error" of gods in flight, from the "dieux qui errent au-dessus de nous" (p. 1482) to "j'ai longtemps erré" (p. 1518) in conjunction with a literal emphasis on duplicity. The infernal presence of "vertu" (p. 1519) which so well pertains to Ulysses' Canto XXVI is followed by the statement, "Je m'arrête," then by, "[J]e me faisais dur," and finally:

> [J]e n'ai jamais pu résisté à l'offre . . . d'une femme.
> (p. 1519)

Such language points directly to the simultaneous presence of the siren and Gorgon, and is followed by a clear statement of the turning around which confirms the immanent threat of petrification, as Clamence speaks of "la face de toutes mes vertus" and "un autre sens . . . un revers." Turning to stone and the Gorgon are recurrent elements of Camus's works as well as the excessive presence of "rain." The context, retrospectively with respect to *La Chute*, suggests the *Commedia*'s rewriting.

Another example of the common process occurs in "Le Minotaure" of *L'Eté*, which includes the infernal connotation as well as "usurers" and "stone":

> Il n'y a plus de déserts. Il n'y a plus d'îles.

This very language is repeated almost word for word in *La Chute*, and a place without islands is a place without Purgatory, condemning its souls to immobilization in the *Inferno*. In "Le Minotaure," Camus qualifies Paris, Prague, Florence, Salzburg, and even Amsterdam as "lieux sans poésie (p. 814), a literal recall of "la morte poesì" which describes the *Inferno*. The same essay associates poetry and stone:

> Pour fuir la poésie et retrouver la paix des pierres, il faut d'autres déserts, d'autres lieux sans âme et sans recours.

The infernal suggestion concretizes itself in the reference to taking no side, immobility, "shade" and "shadows," "walls" evoking the walls of Dis, "Eurydice" and the lyricism of the passage, the "desert," the evocation of the infinite, and the "heart" or "center:" and of course the "invitation" which "one hears from time to time:"

> Mais il y a dans chaque homme un instinct profond qui n'est ni celui de la destruction ni celui de la création. Il s'agit seulement de ne ressembler à rien. A l'ombre des murs chauds d'Oran, sur son asphalte poussiéreux, on entend parfois cette invitation. Il semble que, pour un temps, les esprits qui y cèdent ne soient jamais frustrés. Ce sont les ténèbres d'Eurydice et le sommeil d'Isis. Voici les déserts où la pensée va se répendre, la main fraîche du soir sur un coeur agité . . . . L'esprit rejoint et approuve les Apôtres endormies"
>
> (Camus, "Le Minotaur," *Essais*, p. 830)

Likewise, "Le Mythe de la production" discusses the Gorgon at length. As petrification, stone, and Sisyphus, and the role of the prison cell and confinement play such marked roles in the works prior to *La Chute*, one is lead, particularly through the concept of the latter as a rewriting, to conclude that the *récit* is a synthesis and a destiny, and that the same process takes place within the *récit* itself, as its literal petrifications realize the inversions of the *Inferno* and in the recurrent assimilations by Jean-Baptiste. The black dot on the sea clearly shares a role with the woman who threw herself off the bridge, the siren, the Gorgon, the laughter, Matilda, and the "error" or going off course continues as does Clamence's paradoxical "lyrisme cellulaire."

Let us now return to detect the continuing isotope of Ulysses. Clamence tells more about the barman of Mexico-City:

> Il cambriole, aussi bien, et vous serez surpris d'apprendre que cet homme des cavernes est spécialisé dans le trafic des tableaux. . . . Celui-ci, avec ses airs modestes, est l'auteur du plus célèbres des vols de tableau.
> (pp. 1495-1496)

The world famous theft anticipated concerning that initially visible "empty space on the wall" (p. 1478) has become a realty. Besides, in that very same passage quoted above, Clamence identifies himself as a "counselor" of the people of Amsterdam, in other words, the inferred sailors of Mexico-City as his clientele:

> Je suis le conseiller juridique de ces braves gens. J'ai étudié les lois du pays et je me suis fait une clientèle dans ce quartier où l'on n'exige pas vos diplômes. Ce n'était pas

>   facile, mais j'inspire confiance, n'est-ce pas?
>   J'ai un beau rire franc. . . .
>   (p. 1496)

Since his clients are the clients of Mexico-City, they are necessarily sailors, and Clamence's profession as self-explained above is clearly that of an evil counselor, capable of manipulating words and inspiring confidence--all the while lying. It is also in this passage that Jean-Baptiste has assimilated "laughter" within himself; with respect to this distortion of the siren's song, he is about to assimilate the shipwreck. *Oubli* continues to reign on the literal level of the *récit*, as one approaches another of those nearly metacritical moments in the text, with a repeated insistance on "islands," altitude, and "light," as well as "truth"--all which portray Ulysses' presumption of having reached the Earthly Paradise:

>   On respire mal, l'air est si lourd qu'il pèse
>   sur la poitrine. . . . Comme les canaux sont
>   beaux ce soir! J'aime le souffle des eaux moisies, l'odeur des feuilles mortes qui macèrent
>   dans canal et celle, funèbre, qui monte des
>   péniches pleines de fleurs. . . . La vérité
>   est que je me force à admirer ces canaux. Ce
>   que j'aime le plus au monde c'est la Sicile, vous
>   voyez bien, et encore du haut de l'Etna, dans
>   la lumière, à condition de dominer l'île et
>   la mer. Java, j'y suis allé dans ma jeunesse.
>   D'une manière générale, j'aime toutes les îles.
>   Il est plus facile d'y régner.
>   (pp. 1497-1498)

From the above lines, it is clearly visible that the "heavy air," "stagnant waters," and "autumn leaves," of the opening lines of the *Inferno*, within such proximity of one another, and in the context of the canals of Amsterdam, point directly to the infernal presence. A closer look at this passage shows it as immediately following a reference to Augustinian *obblio*, and the weight of the material world in Clamence's own body and the weight of his own words express, in conjunction with a lack of surefootedness, the appropriate evocation of the whirlwind which condemns Paolo and Francesca:

> Je dois reconnaître cependant que je ne mis plus les pieds sur les quais de Paris. Lorsque j'y passais, en voiture ou en autobus, il se faisait une sorte de silence en moi. . . . Je vis des médecins qui me donnèrent des remontants. Je remontais, et puis redescendais. La vie me devenait moins facile; quand le corps est triste le coeur languit. Il me semblait que je desapprenais en partie ce que je n'avais jamais appris et que je savais pourtant si bien, je veux dire vivre. Oui, je crois bien que c'est alors que tout commença.
> (p. 1497)

The silence, now within Jean-Baptiste, and the fact of climbing and descending, evoke the "silence of the primitive forests" and the "slope" of the first portion of the *récit*, the mark of a beginning point, and here again a beginning point if one permits the deformation of figurative language, repetition, and specificity to realize the Dantesque presence. Clamence also expresses the backwards course and paradox and beginning for a journey. Even the subsequent reference to lack of form is soon to give way to the literal "firm foot"[6] of the *Inferno*'s Canto I or Camus's "pied ferme" (p. 1532):

> Mais ce soir, non plus, je ne me sens pas en en forme. J'ai même du mal à tourner mes phrases. Je parle moins bien, il me semble, et mon discours est moins sûr. Le temps, sans doute. On respire mal. . . .
> (p. 1497)

All those literal marks point to the pigeonholing process of the *Inferno* but succeed in rising to the summit of the presumption of Ulysses' lie, as Clamence verbally flies to the light and the garden of the Earthly Paradise with such excessive insistance on islands. Since he has forced himself to make a choice, which coincides with the expressed lack of desire, another mark of the *Inferno*, one would again most precisely suspect the underlying presence of the Neutral Angels of the Vestibule who are forced to run after a banner. Again, the presence of servitude and the *enseignes* is obsessive, a fact of which the following words are only a brief example:

> Les deux têtes que vous voyez là sont celles
> d'esclaves nègres. Une enseigne. La maison
> appartenait à un vendeur d'esclaves. . . .
> Voilà, j'ai pignon sur rue, je trafique des
> esclaves, je vends de la chair noire." . . .
> L'esclavage, ah, mais non, nous sommes contre!
> (p. 1498)

Between the "two heads," the "flesh," the "slavery," and the famed *enseignes*, familiar elements of the Canto XXXIII are still present in great concentration and continue to amass themselves as follows:

> Aussi, pas d'enseignes, et celle-ci est scanda-
> leuse. D'ailleurs, si tout le monde se mettait
> à table, hein, affichait son vrai métier, son
> identité, on ne saurait plus ou donner de la
> tête! Imaginez des cartes de visite: Dupont,
> philosophe froussard, ou propriétaire chrétien,
> ou humaniste adultère, on a le choix, vraiment.
> Mais ce serait l'enfer! Oui, l'enfer doit être
> ainsi des rues à enseignes et pas moyen de s'ex-
> pliquer. On est classé une fois pour toutes.
> (p. 1499)

From the evil "counselor" to the "stagnant waters," "slavery," and "flesh," Clamence's words finally arrive here at "sitting down at the table" (after a "poisoning"); and once again classification, the "head," and the *enseignes*, lead right to the identity to the *Inferno*: a gradual concretion of sorts continues to function with respect to the rewriting. Likewise, the textual echoes of the *récit* are only too evident.

"Slavery," and *oublis* (pp. 1500-1501) continue to pervade on the literal level and in the subject matter, whose infernal context becomes paradoxically juxtaposed to the salvational one foreseen in the great heights verbally reached by Clamence. Now and besides the paradox reveals itself through an expression which turns the language of the *Paradiso* inside out. The following words express the phenomenon explicitely:

> Quand je m'occupais d'autrui, c'était pure condescendance, en toute liberté, et le mérite entier m'en revenait: je montais d'un degré dans l'amour que je me portais.
> (p. 1500)

"Condescendance," "liberty," "climbing by degrees," and "love" are all perverted. The next lines regard the same parody of language:

> Par degrès, j'ai vu plus clair, . . .
> (p. 1500)

Meanwhile, the infernal "devise de la maison" reads:

> Ne vous y fiez pas.
> (p. 1500)

These words precisely echo the inscription of Dante's Gates of Hell. Similarly, the "seuil de la maison" reads:

> D'où que vous veniez entrez et soyez les bienvenus.
> (p. 1481)

The third instance and last, with respect to the progress of the *récit*, presents itself most explicitly:

> On laisse en y entrant la crainte comme l'espérance.
> (p. 1527)

The three inscriptions are well spread out over the course of the *récit*, and they are a constant reminder of the *Inferno*'s presence and pervading immobility. If one hypothesizes a progression, with respect to the diegesis, the first (p. 1481) is least a reflection of the Dantesque original, since it expresses the betrayal of the welcome guests who find themselves murdered. In the second (p. 1500), the warning is explicit, as duplicity is included in the terms of the statement. The third (p. 1527) is most precisely and literally Dantesque of the three in its reference to "abandon hope." The progress of these three inscriptions follows the movement of the *récit*, as both the inscriptions and the text pigeonhole themselves more and more into the Dantesque identification. Even the final chapter contains a statement by where Clamence asks to be "pigeonholed" (p. 1537) in the "case qui [lui] convient le mieux."

Since the progress of the *récit* parallels the gradual Dantesque pigeonholing process, one may hypothesize the concretion of isotopes on yet another level, in the near and explicit reference to "Dante." After the suggested second inscription, along with the *oublis* and the Augustinian forgetfulness of self, Clamence speaks at great and distorted length on his humiliation during a traffic incident. While these pages refer abundantly to "green" and "red," gradually accumulating heroic language, honking, *courtoisie, gestes*, and Jean-Baptiste's unusual assimilation as he "devours his resentments," the subject matter is disproportionate, both with respect to the rewriting and to the *récit*'s own coherence; but it finds itself in proximity to such explicitly infernal elements, preceded by the presence of numerous isotopes of the rewriting, and eventually interrupted by:

> Tiens, la pluie tombe de nouveau. Arrêtons-nous. . . .
> (p. 1503)

The same paragraph ends with the literal terms of violence, reading novels, and running (p. 1504), and the privileged spot of "rain" to interrupt such a long tirade in conjunction with these elements supports the presence of Ser Brunetto. It is even followed by the mention of "un maître irascible qui voulait, hors de toute loi assommer le délinquant et le mettre à genoux" (p. 1504); the presence of teacher and defiance of the law once again supports the underlying presence of Brunetto Latini. Clamence then interrupts himself again to remark the rain:

> Puisque la pluie redouble et que nous avons le temps, oserais-je vous confier une nouvelle découverte que je fis, peu après, dans ma mémoire? Asseyons-nous à l'abri, sur ce banc. Il y a des siècles que des fumeurs de pipe y contemplent la même pluie tombant sur le même canal.
> (p. 1504)

Even the fact of moving to shelter, recalls the encounter between Dante-pilgrim and his teacher under the rain of fire.

In his perversion, a reference to his rapport with women follows and, within the given context of the rewriting, suggestive of a perverted relationship to Beatrice:

> Je les aimais, selon l'expression consacrée,
> ce qui revient à dire que je n'en ai jamais
> aimé aucune. . . . Cependant, les plaçant si
> haut, je les ai utilisées plus souvent que
> servies. Comment s'y retrouver?
> (p. 1505)

The subject of women and bondage is also a lengthy one, and finally arrives at a statement which asserts once and for all Ulysses' breaking of bonds:

> Mais on ne peut souhaiter la mort de tout le
> monde. Ni, à la limite, dépeupler la planète
> pour jouir d'une liberté inimaginable autrement.
> (p. 1510)

As the subject of bondage continues, Clamence interrupts himself to recover the memory of the original siren incident over the bridge; again the "rain" interrupts Clamence's discourse:

> Tiens, la pluie a cessé!
> (p. 1511)

To this "rain," which plays such a major literal role within the account of a fall, there is the added use of so many terms of Ulysses' Canto XXVI. The final and literal immobility of the incident to which his memory leads him directly precedes Clamence's self-stated plans to leave for an island:

> Je vous mènerai volontiers à l'île. . . .
> (p. 1511)

The passage from the *Inferno*'s last circle to the *Purgatorio*'s shore is recognized by Alfred Cordes.[7] But, particularly as the souls of Amsterdam turn back from the "desert shore" and the "sirens" to "Mexico-City" and its "confusion of languages"

to have a drink in the "last circle"--all such elements are
not so simply read: the light shedded upon them through the
far-reaching echoes of the Ulysses episode make the progress
of Clamence's *récit* a discernible lie.

In the fourth part of the *récit*, Jean-Baptiste leaves for
the island. The passage is finally realized in the text's own
progress, but only partially and verbally realized in the rewriting: Clamence's respect to the *Commedia*, betray him. The
Purgatorio is overwhelmingly present in the evocation of that
second canticle of poetry, *bas-reliefs*, *pierreries*, dreams, *sfumature*, and other characteristic elements of the second canticle,
which make themselves visible in these opening lines of the
récit's fourth part:

> Un village de poupée, ne trouvez-vous pas?
> Le pittoresque ne lui a pas été épargné! Mais
> je ne vous ai pas conduit dans cette île pour
> le pittoresque, cher ami. Tout le monde peut
> vous faire admirer des coiffes, des sabots,
> et des maisons décorées où les pêcheurs
> fument. . . .
>
> (p. 1512)

The above insistance on artifice evokes the *Purgatorio*, but
Clamence will never permit it to remain in this state. He in-
troduces the infernal:

> Nous atteignons la digue. Il faut la suivre
> pour être aussi loin que possible de ces trop
> gracieuses maisons. . . . Voilà, n'est-ce pas,
> le plus beau des paysages négatifs! Voyez,
> à notre gauche, ce tas de cendres qu'on appelle
> ici une dune, la digue grise à notre droite,
> la grève livide à nos pieds et, devant nous,
> la mer couleur de lessive faible, le vaste ciel
> ou se reflètent les eaux blêmes. Un enfer mou,
> vraiment! Rien que des horizontales, aucun
> éclat, l'espace est incolore, la vie morte.
> N'est-ce pas l'effacement universel, le néant

> sensible aux yeux? Pas d'hommes, surtout, pas
> d'hommes! Vous et moi, seulement, devant la
> planète, enfin déserte!
> (p. 1512)

It is clear that Jean-Baptiste has verbally plunged this island into a progressively infernal context, culminating once again in digression, in Ulysses' breaking of bonds with humanity, stagnant waters, repeated lack of color, death, the role of the infinite, "horizontals," and so many forms of negation irreversibly contaminate (or redeem--according to Clamence's inversion) the cleansing process, the shore, and the *sfumature*. Even the role of "horizontals" is an important one, as Jean-Baptiste soon expresses that "the circle of which [he] was the center broke and they all lined up." As Clamence perceives the sand dune as a pile of ashes, the metamorphosis alters any evocation of having reached the shore of an island to the condemnation and precise punishment of Dante's thief, Vanni Fucci:

> Com' el s'accese e arse, e cener tutto
> Convenne che cascando divenisse;
> E poi che fu a terra sì distrutto,
> La polver si raccolse per se stessa,
> E 'n quel medesmo ritornò di butto.
> (*Inferno* XXIV, 101-105)

After all, the theft of a painting plays a major role in the *récit*'s own tale, and one already suspects Jean-Baptiste's complicity along with the stated goal of his evil counseling--to condemn everyone--but, most precisely visible in his assimilation of isotopes, "snakes" ["Après avoir aimé un perroquet, il me fallut coucher avec un serpent" (p. 1524)] mark the process on the part of Clamence, *glisser* passes from the third to first person, and even though the "snake" suggests devilish or medicinal structures, both inherent to the *récit*, the sacred nature of the theft will make itself extensively known within the context of the rewriting, "ashes," "snakes," and the sacred nature of the theft point to another Dantesque presence.

It is at this point in the text that the "doves" previously examined in the context of Paolo and Francesca, as a symbol of desire, make their literal appearance. They lie in an infernal context, but the *Purgatorio* continues to make itself visible throughout. Dante's doves descend in the *Inferno* and scatter in the *Purgatorio*, and Clamence's words do in fact oscillate between the two states--an oscillation which is in perfect accordance with the continued opening words of the *récit*'s fourth part, as they even go so far as to announce the goal to contaminate the initially present *Purgatorio*:

> [L]e ciel . . . s'épaissit, se creuse, ouvre, ferme des portes de nuées. Ce sont les colombes N'avez-vous pas remarqué que le ciel de Hollande est rempli de millions de colombes, invisibles tant elles se tiennent haut, et qui battent des ailes, montent et descendent d'un même mouvement remplissant l'espace céleste avec des flots épais de plumes grisâtres que le vent emporte ou ramène. . . . [J]e perds le fil.
> (p. 1512)

The possible play on words, which insists upon the writing process, is typical of the *Purgatorio*. The movement of the pen filling spaces is clearly present. As Dante traces his own poetic career and synthesizes his own name, he too becomes a "fully feathered poet" during the course of the *Purgatorio*. At the end of the fourth part of the *récit*, in the company of Ulysses' departure and loss of light, Clamence's doves are still paradoxical, as they climb and, at the same time, announce a fall:

> Mais la mer monte, il me semble. Notre bateau
> ne va pas tarder à partir, le jour s'achève.
> Voyez, les colombes se rassemblent là-haut.
> Elles se pressent les unes contre les autres,
> elles remuent à peine, et la lumière baisse.
> Voulez-vous que nous nous taisions pour savourer
> cette heure assez sinistre? Non. . . .
> (p. 1524)

In Ulysses' terms, the above elements announce a shipwreck as well as a moment of revelation; the lie results once again.

The last image of doves in *La Chute* insists upon the loss of feathers and the descent. But also Ugolino's *coucher* finds itself reflected here again to stress the final inversion:

> Voyez les énormes flocons. . . . Ce sont les
> colombes, sûrement. Elles se décident enfin
> à descendre, ces chéries, elles couvrent les
> eaux et les toits d'une épaisse couche de plumes.
> Elles palpitent à toutes les fenêtres. Quelle
> invasion! Espérons qu'elles apportent la bonne
> nouvelle. Tout le monde sera sauvé, et pas
> seulement les élus, les richesses et les peines
> seront partagées et vous, par exemple, à partir
> d'aujourd'hui, vous coucherez toutes les nuits
> sur le sol, pour moi. Toute la lyre, quoi!
> Allons, avouez que vous resteriez pantois si
> un char descendait du ciel pour m'emporter,
> ou si la neige prenait feu. Vous n'y croyez
> pas? Moi non plus.
> (p. 1550)

The language of the *Inferno* situates itself once again with respect to a language of revelation, the *lyre*, poetry, and paradox, culminating in the explicit consciousness of a lie. As the *récit* progressively plunges itself into the fall, a language evoking salvation increasingly forces itself upon the moment. The result is the failure of the lie. Ironically, but logically, it announces the final event of the *récit*, a split, suicide, and decapitation. While serving his head on a platter and jumping into the river, Jean-Baptiste's language abounds in the expression of miracles, salvation, and reflection, as he ironically assimilates the final terms of Ugolino's and Ulysses' tale, the perversion of the Word, and the plunge. Having turned inverse reasoning into the "right direction," Clamence has succeeded in realizing a split, which destroys him as well as finding itself concretized in his decapitation.

Returning to the fourth division of the *récit*, one continues to detect the presence of Ulysses:

> Je n'ai que des complices.
>   (p. 1513)

The statement confirms the relationship between Ulysses and Diomedes in their theft of the Palladium. It is soon thereafter that Clamence refers to "Dante" and his "Neutral Angels," a reference which, with respect to proximity and the notion of gradual concretion, confirms the question of the above complexity as Dantesque in nature. The only truly metacritical passage of the *récit* is as follows and echoes the synthesis of the "last circle:" "Vous savez cela? Diable. . . ." (p. 1483):

> Connaissez-vous Dante? Vraiment? Diable.
> Vous savez donc que Dante admet des anges
> neutres dans la querelle entre Dieu et Satan.
> El il les place dans les Limbes, une sorte de
> vestibule de son enfer. Nous sommes dans le
> vestibule, cher ami.
>   (p. 1518)

A closer look at the above elements shows the presence of the "vestibule" not to be alone. While elements of Dante's Vestibule or Neutral Angels are undeniable within the *récit* and logically lead to their concretized validity above, the above words also place them in Limbo, therefore identifying it with the circle of Dante's Virtuous Heathens as well as with Canto XXI of the *Purgatorio*. It is in the latter that Dante-pilgrim learns of Statius' ironic conversion to Christianity thanks to his misreading of Virgil. "Laughter" plays a marked role at this point in the *Commedia*, even more prevalent than in the Earthly Paradise where it concerned Matilda. In Canto XXII of the *Purgatorio*,

> 'Perchè non reggi tu, o sacra fame
> De l'oro, l' appetitio de' mortali?'
> (*Purgatorio* XXII, 40-41)

Statius is placed on the fifth terrace among the avaricious but is actually guilty of prodigality.[8] The line Statius quotes must be misinterpreted, not read in terms of the "hunger for gold" but in terms of the "sacred hunger" or "natural thirst for spiritual nourishment" (see Pézard's footnote to the verse).

Soon after *La Chute*'s only mention of "Dante," Clamence discourses on the subject of his clients and the roles they play when taking a firm stand, often where money is of principal concern. Not taking a stand is obviously the error of Dante's Neutral Angels, but then Clamence refers to "celui qui parlait d'or" (p. 1527), and Virgil's verses supply the clearest continuity for the rewriting. Forcing oneself to "take a side" (p. 1498) or to "play a role" (p. 1526) is a term of the sequence which announces the Neutral Angels of Dante's Vestibule, but it remains a fact that Camus refers specifically to "les Limbes." Camus would never have made such an error as to confuse the circle of the Virtuous Heathens, where Virgil resides, and the Vestibule. Even though Jean-Baptiste will soon say, "Je trône parmi mes vilains anges" (p. 1549), which clarifies the identification of the Vestibule one step further and ties up the recurrent *trôner* of Camus's previous works into the isotopes of the rewriting to equate Clamence and Lucifer, Virtuous Heathens, another of those categories associated with flames and blasphemy, are close at hand within *La Chute*.

Clamence then assimilates "error" in conjunction with duplicity, which justifies all the more our deformation of the following words:

[J]'ai longtemps erré.
(p. 1518)

The subsequent subject matter of Greek islands is of course completely logical in the sequence provided by Dante's anti-hero:

> Dans l'archipel grec, j'avais l'impression contraire. Sans cesse de nouvelles îles apparaissaient sur le cercle de l'horizon. Leur échine sans arbres traçait la limite du ciel, leur rivage rocheux tranchait nettement sur la mer. Aucune confusion; dans la lumière précise, tout était repère. Et d'une île à l'autre, sans trêve, sur notre petit bateau, qui se traînait pourtant, j'avais l'impression de bondir, nuit et jour, à la crête des courtes vagues fraîches, dans une course pleine d'écume et de rires. Depuis ce temps, la Grèce elle-même dérive quelque part en moi, au bord de ma mémoire, inlassablement... Eh! la, je dérive, moi

> aussi, je deviens lyrique! Arrêtez-moi, cher,
> je vous en prie.
> (p. 1525)

Here, as before, the islands are going off course, and a shipwreck is in the making and all the more emphasized by the presence of the "rocky shore," the "rires," the twice occurring *dériver*, the evocation of the infinite, the "cercle" the "traçait la limite," the "tranchait," the "horizon," and the "arrêtez-moi" in conjunction with the lyricism lead once again to the equivalence between going off course and words, all within the context of Ulysses' voyage and its thematically repeated elements throughout *La Chute*. The above words most precisely express the sea-going voyage in terms of a flight. Even the paragraph to follow the above one makes reference to "Greece" and to "women staying at home," which are other precise marks of Ulysses' story. The break with humanity and the siren-Gorgon-Beatrice figure of a lady make themselves heard:

> Je décidai de quitter la société d'hommes. . . .
> [L]a femme est la récompense . . . du criminel.
> Elle est son port, son havre, c'est dans le
> lit de la femme qu'il est généralement arrêté.
> (p. 1526)

The subsequent reference to the loss of islands, along with the above elements, results in the same course as that seen at the end of the first part of the *récit*. As going off course evokes a shipwreck, in which the islands are moving, the break with humanity and the call of this multiple figure of a woman produce the extreme paradox which is confirmed in the following lines:

> N'est-elle pas tout ce qui nous reste du paradis
> terrestre? Desemparé, je courus à mon port
> naturel. . . . [J]e fis la bête.
> (p. 1526)

The Earthly Paradise, the natural port, and the woman, have nothing infernal about them and are suited perfectly to Dante's language. But here, they find themselves in the context of the "error" or going off course, and the final transformation into an animal concretizes the preceding use of *arrêter* or immobility so often in the final position of the echoed structures, is surely a mark of Ulysses' Circe, the siren who lured him off the straight path and changed men into beasts, and the subject of the first line of his dramatic monologue in Canto XXVI.

Clamence's flight of language continues to be so often expressed in terms of the sea-going voyage as well as the successful flight. Here is another example stressing the progress of this pilgrimage wth the progress of the *récit*, again a mark of Dante's poem:

> Je vivais encore de mon métier, quoique ma réputation fut bien entamée par mes écarts de langage. . . . Ma propre voix m'entraînait, je la suivais; sans vraiment planer, comme autrefois, je m'élevais. . . .
> (p. 1530)

For the next and last twenty pages of the *récit*, Ulysses presence is so overwhelming, not so much in terms of adding specificity as in mass and repetition of previously seen elements, that it is perhaps more constructive to dwell upon precisions and his assimilation of the terms involved. He finally and explicitly tells his listener that his own clients are sailors:

> Il y en a beaucoup dans le monde, mais le hasard, la commodité, l'ironie, et la nécessité aussi d'une certaine mortification, m'ont fait choisir une capitale d'eaux et de brumes, corsetée de canaux, particulièrement encombrée, et visitée par des hommes venus du monde entier. J'ai installé mon cabinet dans un bar du quartier des matelots. La clientèle des ports est diverse. . . . Je guette . . . le bourgeois qui s'égare. . . . Je tire de lui, en virtuose, les accents les plus raffinés.
> (p. 1547)

The infernal context is of course a major factor in the identification; the emphasis on the canals, the waters, and the diversity of languages, and the snobbery of refined languages-- all are elements shown to be suspiciously working towards the concretion of those presented by the isotope in the first portion of the *récit*, in the barman's disdain of the civilized languages and in the reception of sailors of all nationalities until repetition, specificity, and density further realized our suspicions concerning the anti-hero's role. The following paragraph is a long and continued lecture on evil counseling, followed by the image of Jean-Baptiste covered with ashes:

> Couvert de cendres, m'arrachant lentement les cheveux, . . . je me tiens devant l'humanité entière.
> (p. 1547)

While Ulysses' thievery concerns us most, the isotopic mark belongs most precisely to Vanni Fucci. The above language proves once again the capacity of Jean-Baptiste to assimilate all isotopes of the Dantesque presence, a phenomenon further supported by the fact that earlier in the *récit*, he imagined a dune to be a pile of ashes. (Even though the *récit*'s own coherence verbally reveals the same assimilation of "ashes," the significance is clearly lacking.) Such further properties of the terms of the sequence are futher supported by Clamence's assimilation of "snakes," and *glisser*:

> J'assenais ce maître mot servitude. . . . Je le glisserai. . . .
> (p. 1543-1544)

The importance of this language is further emphasized by yet another instance of its assimilation:

> Je glisserai là-dessus, . . .
> (P. 1529)

From the presence of the "snake," with whom Jean-Baptiste went to bed in his perversion of love (such violence belongs equally to Brunetto's sodomy as to Vanni Fucci), to the *glisser* of the third person, to the two twice occurring assimilation of *glisser*, a process of engulfment clearly continues to be realized with specific respect to Dante's thief.

The sacred nature of the theft (p. 1542) then comes into play at length. In the next to last paragraph of the *récit*, Ulysses stresses again the fact of being an accomplice, this time in reference to himself and regarding the theft, which indicates and pinpoints his assimilation of the relationship of "complicity" with Diomedes:

> J'espère toujours, en effet, que mon interlocuteur sera policier et qu'il m'arrêtera pour le vol des Juges intègres. Pour le reste, n'est-pas, personne ne peut m'arrêter. Mais quant à ce vol, il tombe sous le coup de la loi et j'ai tout arrangé pour me rendre complice; je recèle ce tableau et le montre à qui veut le

voir. Vous m'arrêteriez donc. . . .
(pp. 1550-1551)

Within the given context, the continued literal emphasis on *arrêter* and *vol* plays again upon Ulysses' fall, which is rendered all the more ironic in the simile of Elijah in Canto XXVI. Similarly, Jean-Baptiste envisions himself as the same successful hero:

Je suis . . . Elie sans Messie. . . .
(p. 1535)

The final assimilation concerning the Ulysses isotope occurs in the final part of the *récit*. Clamence has finally assimilated the fall, undertaken it himself to the point of the literal plunge, an insistence upon the infinite, the disdain, flattery and evil counseling and words, the complicity, and the call of his siren-Gorgon-Eurydice-Beatrice figure of a lady:

> Je savais que nous étions de la même race. Ne sommes-nous pas tous semblables, parlant sans trêve et à personne, confrontés toujours aux mêmes questions bien que nous connaissions d'avance les réponses? Alors, racontez-moi, je vous prie, ce qui vous est arrivé un soir sur les quais de la Seine et comment vous avez réussi à ne jamais risquer votre vie. Prononcez vous même les mots qui, depuis des années n'ont cessé de retentir dans mes nuits, et que je dirai enfin par votre bouche; "O jeune fille, jette-toi encore dans l'eau pour que j'aie une seconde fois la chance de nous sauver tous les deux!" Une seconde fois, hein, quelle imprudence! Supposez, cher maître, qu'on nous prenne au mot? Il faudrait s'exécuter. Brr...! l'eau est si froide! Mais rassurons-nous! Il est trop tard, maintenant, il sera toujours trop tard. Heureusement!
> (p. 1551)

As Clamence insists on "being of the same race" in conjunction with speaking "ceaselessly and to no one," we are brought literally back to those first lines of the *récit* in which we detected the presence of Dante's Ulysses in the inverse "disdain of the civilized languages." Similarly, the immobility of Clamence's last words is evoked through their own coherence, in the fact of nothing having happened, as illustrated by the immobility of being confronted "toujours aux mêmes questions bien que nous connaissions d'avance les réponses" and the "il sera toujours trop tard:" the *toujours déjà* factor situates Clamence's *récit* in the immobility of a paradoxical discourse, the evocation of the inside out immobility of the *Inferno* as well as the *Paradiso*'s final vision of those infinite circles which are inversely proportionate to the ones first sighted at the moment of the beatific vision, ending in Dante-pilgrim's underwater point of view as "All'alta fantasia qui manco possa" (*Paradiso* XXXIII, 142). The circularity is also reflected in the syntactical reflections: at the end of the first part of the *récit*, in the context of numerous elements of Dante's Ulysses' isotope, Jean-Baptiste "supposed" a cold-water-plunge to save someone, and his state evoked one of paradox, miracles, and elation in response to the call of women, the going off course, the islands where men die happy and insance, the last circle, and the final optimism of shipwreck. The very last word of the *récit* is "Heureusement," evoking within the reflected and circular context those "îles où les hommes meurent fous et heureux" in conjunction with the sea-going voyage, error, and the descent of gods; therefore, even the *récit*'s own coherence reveals to some extent the immobility, circularity, and reflection through the very same literal terms which constitute Dante's Ulysses' isotope and the lie discerned through the rewriting: Clamence maintains the paradox, the miracle, and the attainment of the infinite to the very end--and beyond.

In order to further ascertain the assimilation of the plunge, it is most appropriate to include Ugolino's isotope: the importance of words, the mouth, the cold, the immobilization, the sacrifice, and the literal meaning of words--all are elements of the above passage. As Jean-Baptiste assimilates his client in the above words with respect to reflections, the *même*, and even to the point of speaking through his client's mouth, he insists on words, literally on the word *mot*, as he assimilates what was once another's figurative fall and supposes the fact of "being taken literally" in his plunge. Ugolino's underlying presence supports our literal reading of these words, as the indices of his account in Canto XXXIII lead us to take him literally in his cannibalism.

Before leaving the process of assimilation, one should note Clamence's assimilation regarding the separation of language and meaning whose inversion he has undertaken. It was clear that the image of the people of Holland with their heads in neon clouds and other elevated places depicted a sort of decapitation. Then it became evident that the Augustinian split from the self was another source of separation in the figurative sense, as is the straying from the straight path in "error." The use of *couper*, most often in the context of judgement, as in the *Commedia*, is of high frequency in Camus's text (pp. 1478, 1487, 1514, 1522, and 1545); the figurative usage succeeds in passing to the literal level as Jean-Baptiste refers to the "misfortune of cutting oneself" (p. 1515). Likewise, Clamence always attempts the inversion of the meaning of words or their *sens* or direction, his stated goal within the text's own coherence as well as one of the rewriting's results. In the next to last paragraph of the *récit*, Jean-Baptiste literally serves his head on a platter, the decapitation is at least verbally successful, the reasoning is inverted, and the fall is inevitable. The excessive *têtes* and *bouches* of the *récit* are also constant marks of the final literal and physical separation, just as they are marks of the *Inferno*, particularly the last circle, and of course of John the Baptist. Likewise, the "devouring," "taste," "rumination," "mouthfuls," "heads," "hosts," and "chewing" of the *récit* succeeded in occupying more and more text until the last pages where they extend themselves into a relatively lengthy metaphor: "Mais il était trop tard, et je dévorai pendant quelques jours un vilain ressentiment" (p. 1503); "ils allaient me dévorer" (p. 1515); "[s]ans elle, [la "servitude"] à vrai dire, il n'y a point de solution définitive. J'ai très vite compris cela. Autrefois, je n'avais que la liberté à la bouche. Je l'étendais au petit déjeuner sur mes tartines, je la mastiquais toute la journée, je portais dans le monde une haleine délicieusement rafraîchie à la liberté" (pp. 1543-1544). As for the omnipresent *bouche* of the *récit*, its literal occurrence also becomes progressively magnified into that last prophecy of the last paragraph in which Clamence asks his client, "Prononcez vous-même les mots qui, depuis des années, n'ont cessé de retentir dans mes nuits, et que *je dirai enfin par votre bouche.*" (my emphasis).

To the above, let us also add the coexistence of isotopes, paradox, a language which suggests the underlying presence of a cleansing process and the movement towards the beatific vision--all working progressively to intensify themselves with respect to the progress of the *récit* by making use of the discernment of the rewriting's density, mass, specificity, and repetition. The increasing expression of paradox, miracles, geometrical language, the *sauver* accumulating aphorisms, and isotopic formation with insistance on the lie and the eventual realization of the punishment with respect to the *Commedia* point to the resulting and definitive split and announce the precipitation of fall. Just as the assimilation of isotopes takes place principally in the fifth and sixth divisions of the *récit*, Ugolino's parody of the Word made Flesh takes place in the account of the passage from the fifth to sixth day of his torment, and the result is a split in meaning, recalling the split which Clamence has hopefully succeeded in undertaking. The passage from the fifth to the sixth is curiously of some importance for Jean-Baptiste: his method of separating words from their meaning uses six ennumerated steps and stresses the final separation (p. 1542); he refers to five years in Paris followed by death (p. 1545); and he refers to having been five days with his client after which "la chute se produit à l'aube" (p. 1549). Such evidence therefore occurs in the last moments of *La Chute*, just as it occurs in the last moments of Ugolino's account. One is lead to conclude the inversion of the Word.

Footnotes to Chapter III

[1] By "the literal to the literal," I mean that the words involved in the disfigurement have no figurative usage, which is often the case: for example, islands are always islands, but they can have a literal meaning which is not to be taken in its physical sense, as seen on page 1483. As for the process of mythologization: "Melville a construit ses symboles sur le concret, non dans le matériau du rêve. Le créateur de mythes ne participe au génie que dans la mesure oú il les inscrit dans l'épaisseur de la réalité et non dans les nuées fugitives de l'imagination" (Albert Camus, "Herman Melville," *Theâtre, récits, nouvelles*, p. 1909).

[2] "Ma l' orbita che fe la parte somme/Si sua circunferenza e derelitta,/Si ch' e la muffa dov' era la gromma" (*Paradiso* XII, 112-114).

[3] "E disser: "Padre, assai ci fia men doglia/Se tu mangi di noi: tu ne vestisti/Queste misere carni, e tu le spoglia'" (*Inferno* XXXIII, 61-63).

[4] "Lethe is in the lower world of the ancients; but Dante puts it in the Garden of Eden, at the top of the mountain of Purgatory" (E. Ciafardini, "L'idrografia dell' *inferno* e del *purgatorio* dantesco," *Studii in onore di Francesco Torraca* [1922], p. 260, quoted in C. H. Grandgent, "*La divina commedia*" *di Dante Alighieri* [Boston: D.C. Heath and Company, 1933], p. 134).

[5] Tzvetan Todorov, "Le Récit primitif; l'Odyssée," *Poétique de la prose* (choix) (Paris: Editions du Seuil, 1971) pp. 21-32.

[6] "Po che' ei posato un poco il corpo lasso,/Ripresi via per la piaggia diserta,/Si che 'l piè fermo sempre era 'l più basso." (*Inferno* I, 29-31); Freccero, "Firm Foot." *Studii danteschi*, Vol. XXXIX.

[7] Alfred Cordes, *The Descent of the Doves: Camus's Journey to the Spirit* (Washington, D.C.: University Press of America, 1960), p. 147.

[8] *In Dante sous la pluie de feu*, Pézard points out the parallel between Brunetto and Statius, insofar as Brunetto is not really guilty of sodomy nor Statius of avarice: "Stace fut prodigue, et la terrace qu'il traverse punit la prodigalité à égal du péché contraire" (p. 24).

Conclusions

The hypothesized existence of *La Chute* as rewritten by the *Commedia* proves itself a valid means of understanding, intensifying, and synthesizing much of the *récit*; therefore, its proven practical method of reading succeeds in unifying Jean-Baptiste's words and gives meaningful perspective to them without claiming to substitute itself for the text's own coherence. Further realizing it as it ties up its literal elements through additional structures, the rewriting further synthesizes its *littérarité*, one of the many results of the *Commedia*'s working with and against the *récit* taken in the full sense of its "multiplicity of possible translations."

The first paragraph of Jean-Baptiste Clamence's account provides some of the clearest, simplest, and most important examples of the double perspective, as the process enhances what is already working within the text's own coherence to a large extent. Within the latter, the gorilla-barman-host's disdain of the civilized languages, Mexico-City within Amsterdam, the primitive forests of the host's silence, and the Cro-Magnon "pensionnaire à la tour de Babel" provide a contradiction and/or an element out of place; but the added perspective of the rewriting sees the clear inversion of Ulysses' disdain of the vulgar languages, a similar beginning point for the voyages of both Clamence-pilgrim headed downward and Dante-pilgrim, Cocytus within Amsterdam, a heroic parody of Nimrod as a Cro-Magnon locked in the tower, and suggestions of other

Dantesque presences. The undercutting becomes all the more powerful and proves itself valid, since our suspicions are so very often confirmed on the literal level of the *récit* through the isotopes of the rewriting, as we pass from the suggestion to its precision. So often, as the rewriting confirms its own validity through the existence of isotopes, clear characteristics of the *récit*'s own language are intensified to include the extension of literal meaning to produce Clamence's perceptions of the world, inversions, duplicity, and even the role of Dante and a theological perspective; and of course all the elements which lead to the formation of isotopes are already literal elements of Camus's text: all the rewriting does is synthesize them into narratives, as repetition, density, and specificity (including context and proximity) are the tools for the discernment of these structures.

The rewriting also demonstrates the abstract immobilization of the recurrent elements of Camus's previous writings through the concretion of its various Dantesque isotopes, which again leads one to view the *récit* as a synthesis and precipitation. As seen within *La Chute* itself, the deformation of figurative language is also active in this vision of the *récit* as an end point with respect to Camus's previous works, and of course most active within *La Chute* as a rewriting. Likewise, while Dante's *Inferno*, by the time we reach Cocytus, increasingly has set itself in Holland for the contemporary reader, dikes and windmills are recurrent elements of Camus's texts but never occur in the Netherlands until *La Chute*; thus,

the geographical "negation" also appears as a destiny; within
La Chute itself and made apparent through the rewriting, Amsterdam echoes the infernal traits of Paris, and the "illusions,"
"shades," "autumn leaves," "rain," and circular motion are all
recurrent elements of Camus's earlier decors of North Africa,
South America, and New York. Furthermore and retrospectively,
the juxtaposition of certain elements in written works preceding *La Chute* creates infernal narratives, as "heavy air,"
"rain," "forests," "hills," "shores," "boats," "crossings,"
"sirens," "madness," "persuasion," "islands," and "classification"--just to name a few--delineate the world which gives way
to the *Inferno* of *La Chute* and foreshadow the synthesis of its
Dantesque isotopes. Similarly, the symbol of the flame, a mark
of unifying blasphemy, which links the usurers and sodomites
under the rain of fire, Ulysses, Pope Nicholas, the thieves,
the hypocrites, the virtuous heathens, and all those subject
to light in some form or another and to whom the corrective
is offered in the subsequent canticles, reveals itself in the
blasphémateurs of *L'Homme révolté*, who also find themselves situated under a "rain of fire." As such examples illustrate the
fact that Camus's previous works are capable of further
realizing the isotopes of *La Chute* rewritten, the latter's incessant rain, along with its "usurers," and the isotopic existence of Ser Brunetto, Ulysses, and Pope Nicholas III--to
name the clearest--appears more justifiably and more completely Dantesque, through the naming of the *blasphémateurs*
under a "rain of fire." Also, the rain of "Pluies de New

York" is more specifically infernal than the rain of *La Chute*, while the former remains more intertextual than isotopic. To the above examples, one must add the petrification inferred from the rewriting, as it plays such a literal role in previous works: the "gorgon," the *regard*, and "stone" are among such recurrent elements. Other obsessional and retrospectively possibly Dantesque elements include the references to the middle of life, prison cells, doves which circle, loss of memory, and the *enseignes*: *La Chute*, at least to some degree, is a synthesis.

While the above overview may set the stage for the hypothesized rewriting, the principal focus of our hypothesis has been the confirmation of isotopes over the course of the *récit* without taking into account preceding works. The Dantesque narratives succeed in illustrating the force of an abstract and immobilizing presence through the proven validity of a deformed reading. While cumulative formation of an isotope is enough to concretize it, a gradual increase in density and specificity of elements which lend themselves to the formation of the Dantesque isotopes demonstrates most conclusively the rewriting's validity and the gradual tendency towards immobilization. The identifications of Cocytus and Ulysses clearly are the two examples, which develop out of vague hints, then through increasing specificity and eventually to those massively and densely rewritten passages of the end of the *récit*'s first part, leaving their pervading traits to characterize both globally and specifically the remainder of the *récit*. On the other hand, Ugolino and Pope Nicholas III, without accounting for large portions of the text, are most convincing in the progression from hint to precision--that is, from intertextuality to isotope. Present throughout the *récit*, they engender much of its less poetic and more eventful specificity, a sign in itself of immobilization as the deformations required by the rewriting link elements which would remain otherwise far removed from one another and dislodge elements from the text's coherence into the isotopes which so often arrive at a precise statement of the *contrapasso* and the lie which characterizes the blindness of the inhabitants of the *Inferno*. Apart from the proven validity of the rewriting, the majority of our evidence leads to this important conclusion. Such is the case with Pope Nicholas, stuck upside down in a rocky funnel, in the parody of San Giovanni's baptismal font, as future corrupt Popes will take his palce and push him further into the rocky crevices; Ugolino immobilized and locked in the ice up to his neck, chewing, wiping, and literally attached to the jailor who locked him in the tower, an invention of the Middle Ages, to starve to death; Paolo and Francesca in the whirlwind of passion and unable to descend; the lie of Ser Brunetto who taught man how to be eternal through literature; the lie of Ulysses to persuade his men to break all bonds with humanity in the pursuit of virtue and knowledge without divine guidance, to undertake the sea-going voyage expressed in terms of a successful flight to the summit of his presumption, and thematically important roles of the sea, shores, summits, island, and the call of the siren. On a less extensive isotopic scale, Nimrod's heroic parody has him resemble a tower, and capable of sounding a horn; the rain of fire condemns usurers and Ser Brunetto; the Neutral Angels run in circles with no hope of death, since they made no choice in the quarrel between Satan and God; and the metamorphosis of the thieves from snake to ashes. While many intertextual references never prove their Dantesque existence beyond the shadow of a hint, others extend themselves slightly beyond, and still others are precise identifications met in passing but which go little or no further than the mention of "Neutral Angels," "Dante," "prostitutes," the Gate's inscriptions to "abandon all hope," and "usurers;" however, they are elements which reinforce and create the context and the interpretations of the rewriting to include rain, loss of memory, laughter, rivers, ladies, islands, summits, descending doves, forests, hosts, virtue, inscriptions resembling those of the Gates of Hell, camel hair dress, hooves, rumination, justice, John the Baptist, towers, courtly literature, Elijah, circular motion, *fornicateurs* and *lecteurs* and whirlwinds, locked doors, the wish to be eternal and literature, and all elements, no matter how vague or precise with respect to the Dantesque context provided and which lend themselves to the often plural possibilities of the rewriting. Among the more extensive presences cited previously in the entirety of their narratives, it is the *contrapasso* and the lie which come to exist most predominantly through the formation of the rewriting's isotopes.

After all, these Dantesque characters could have revealed themselves through other elements, but the isotopic insistance always revealed itself through the reversals inherent to the *contrapasso* and the lie, therefore stressing that quality which is already present within *La Chute*'s own coherence, in the irony, the ability of literal meaning to engender subsequent language, Clamence's own preoccupation with words, their *sens*, and Clamence's own stated goal to invert that "direction" and "meaning." As we are invited to share in Ugolino's guilt of literal cannibalism, and accordingly to follow Jean-Baptiste's words through the "last circle," through physical immobilization in a tower and a locked room, an invention of Middle Ages, along with "wiping," "sticking" to one's jailor, and eventually a statement to invert the meaning of words, one logically arrives at the literal fall of the final plunge.

Another trait of the rewriting is the movement towards immobilization and death, as revealed in Jean-Baptiste's ability or destiny to realize and assimilate so many of the isotopes of the rewriting within himself--that is, to his first person discourse, even equating himself at one instance with the "last circle" in "Là, je les attends", which also proves the directing force of both the first and last portions of the *récit*. Such a pattern of engulfment is perhaps most specific, convincing, and conclusive as enhanced by the concept of *La Chute* as a rewriting. We see Ugolino's isotope illustrate the syndrome through the use of "sticking" and *couché*, which both pass to the first person of the *récit*. Similarly, Clamence arrives at a point where he states his own "going off course." But hte clearest example of Clamence's assimilation and the passage from the intertextual suggestion to isotopic precision is Pope Nicholas III: from the *coincé* of the reference to the people of Holland, then more precisely isotopic to the *coincé* of upside down people in rocky funnels whom Jean-Baptiste hates, and finally to the *coincé* of Clamence himself and the completion of his isotope's required specificity as he comes to describe himself as being *coincé* in a baptismal font and having been elected Pope in a time before the present one. This most precise of examples therefore illustrates the isotope's formation as taking place purely in the language of Clamence's account, in spite of place, time, and intent. Through one simple adjective, we are able to follow that progress from the vague hint to increasing precision of context, which gives birth to the Dantesque identification, Clamence's assimilation, and the *contrapasso*.

Transformed into the hero of an anti-voyage (in the positive sense), Ulysses provides the most extensive isotope with respect to density, specificity, and mass, as "madness," "sirens," "happiness," "islands," a call to leave the world, flight, and so many other elements of primarily poetic interest with respect to Clamence's words alone, find themselves caught into the narrative thread which links them to the disdain of languages, the theft of a sacred art object, evil counseling, shipwreck, the plunge, Elijah, and other precise elements of the Dantesque sequence. The reading which does not make use of Ulysses' isotope overlooks these elements in a poetic sense or as a part of Camus's myth-making world; but whether it is in the figurative to the literal, or the literal to another literal meaning, or myth to reality, a deformation, inversion, and the concretion of an isotope occurs to anticipate the "dead poetry" of the *Inferno*, the final plunge, and a parody of the Word. To these distortions, one should add Camus's evil counselor's characteristic use of aphorisms, again the abstraction of an immobilization.

Another twist occurs in the overwhelming contamination by elements of the *Purgatorio* and the *Paradiso*, whose slightest hints at unity, revelation, cleansing, lyricism, movement towards a point where words no longer mask reality, the *paradoxisme* which expresses a truer approximation of reality, and images such as these of fish rising to the surface to eat, natural hunger, natural thirst, reflections, camel dress, rumination, rivers and loss of memory, light, circles and lines, laughter, gardens, islands, the call of a female figure, and the final plunge--all succeed in confusing the infernal issue. Jean-Baptiste always succeeds in confusing the revelation of paradox with the duplicity of lie and of a language which masks reality. Even the figurative fall of language is reflected in the recurrent image of the backwards movement from the *Purgatorio*'s desert shore back to the *Inferno*'s last and icy circle. Its traits and categories significantly direct the *récit*'s first portion as well as its last, through Treachery, Hosts, the "last circle," towers, exile, babble, poisonings at the table, physical immobilization, cold, the question of taking words literally, the parody of meaning, and the fiction of having reached a point of conversion, crossing, etc.... The direction of the deepest and most central realm of the *Inferno*, Earth, or Jean-Baptiste, turns into the right one. Similarly, almost all infernal elements of the rewriting are lyrical, and just as frequent is the duality or multiplicity which concerns rivers (Phlegyas/Lethe), female figures and their call (the siren/gorgon/Beatrice), forests and gardens (the Dark Wood/the Wood of the Suicides/the Earthly Paradise) summits (Ulysses' presumption/the *Purgatorio*), shores, dreams, ocean voyages, flights, islands, the plunge, and countless other terms which lend themselves to the *Commedia*'s thematic echoes and corrective processes, as well as to the duality of the rewriting and collapse of language.

The more one reads *La Chute* and previous works, the more *imaginaire* the notion of a rewriting becomes, if one allows for recurrent elements to supply the most concrete structural building blocks; but even as the case may be, the rewriting works within *La Chute* to concretize and synthesize Camus's language from within *La Chute* or from outside it.

La Chute has been shown, through its manuscripts, to be the most worked over of any of Camus's writings; each subsequent version reveals the language of the *récit* to be further and further rooted into the symbolic and mythological. This factor supports all the more the hypothesis that *La Chute* is most fully realized in its *littérarité* as it works harder and synthesizes the often obsessional elements of Camus's fictional world and/or even his real one.

Bibliography

Adam, Jean-Michel. *Linguistique et discours littéraire: théorie et pratique des textes.* Paris: Librairie Larousse, 1976.

Albert Camus 3 (1970) sur "La Chute". Texts reunited under the direction of Brian Fitch in *La Revue des lettres modernes,* Nos. 238-244 (1970).

Albert Camus 1980. Proc. of the Second International Conference. 21-23 Feb. 1980. Edited by Raymond Gay-Crosier. Gainesville: University of Florida, 1980.

Archambault, Paul. "Albert Camus et la métaphysique chrétienne," in *Albert Camus 1980.* Proc. of the Second International Conference. 21-13 Feb. 1980. Edited by Raymond Gay-Crosier. Gainesville: University of Florida, 1980.

----------. "Augustin et Camus." *Recherches augustiennes,* 6 (1969).

----------. *Camus's Hellenic Sources.* Chapel Hill: Universtiy of North Carolina Press, 1972.

Azzioni, Terreni. "Camus face aux mythes." *Culture française,* pp. 211-214.

Barchilon, Jose. *"The Fall* by Albert Camus. A psychoanalytical study." *International Journal of Psychoanalysis,* No. 49 (1968), pp. 386-389.

----------. "A study of Camus's Mythopoetic Tale, *The Fall,* with Some Comments About the Origin of Esthetic Feelings." *Journal of the American Psychoanalytical Association,* No. 19 (1971), pp. 193-240.

Blanchot, Maurice. "La Confession dédaigneuse." *La Nouvelle revue française,* (dec. 1965).

----------. *Le Livre à venir.* Paris: Gallimard, collection Idées, 1959.

Bloom, Harold. *The Anxiety of Influence.* New York: Oxford University Press, 1973.

----------. *A Map of Misreading.* New York: Oxford University Press, 1975.

Brockman, Charles. "Metamorphoses of Hell: the Spiritual Quandary in *La Chute." French Review,* No. 35 (1962), pp. 361-368.

Camus, Albert. *Carnets I: mai 1935-fév. 1942.* Paris: Gallimard, 1962.

----------. *Carnets II: janvier 1942-mars 1951.* Paris: Gallimard, 1964.

----------. *Essais.* Paris: Gallimard, Bibliothèque de la Pléiade, 1967.

----------. *Théâtre, récits, nouvelles.* Texts annotated by Roger Quillot. Paris: Gallimard, Bibliothèque de la Pléiade, 1962.

Chiampi, James Thomas. *Shadowy Prefaces: Conversion and Writing in the "Divine Comedy".* Ravenna: Longo editore, 1981.

Clayton, A. J. "Note sur Augustin et Camus." *La Revue des lettres modernes* (1972), pp. 315-322.

Freccero, John. "Dante's Firm Foot and the Journey without a Guide." *The Harvard Theological Review* 52 (1959), pp. 245-288.

----------. "Dante's Prologue Scene." *Dante Studies,* 84 (1966), 1-27.

----------. "Dante's Ulysses; from Epic to Novel," in *Concepts of the Hero in the Middle Ages and the Renaissance.* Papers of the fourth and fifth annual conferences of the Center for Medieval and Early Renaissance Studies. Edited by Norman T. Burns and Christopher J. Reagan. Albany State University: New York Press, 1975, pp. 101-119.

----------. "Infernal Inversion and Christian Conversion (*Inferno* XXXIV)." *Italica,* 42 (1965), 35-41.

Gassin, Jean. *L'Univers symbolique d'Albert Camus: essai d'interprétation psychanalytique.* Paris: Librairie Minard, 1981.

Genette, Gérard. *Palimpsestes: la littérature au second degré.* Paris: Editions du Seuil, collection Poétique, 1982.

Grandgent, C. H., ed. and annotator. *"La divina commedia" di Dante Alighieri.* Boston: D. C. Heath and Company, 1933.

Lansing, Richard. *From Image to Idea: a Study of the Simile in Dante's "Commedia".* Ravenna: Longo Editore, 1976.

La Vallée, Williams. "Biblical Allusions in *La Chute*." *A Journal in the Humanities and Social Sciences,* 2, No. 2 (1973), pp. 13-31.

McCarthy, Patrick. *Camus*. New York: Random House, 1982.

Petry, Sandy. "The Function of Christian Imagery in *La Chute*." *Texas Studies in Literature and Language: A Journal of the Humanities*, 11 (1970), 145-154.

Pézard, André, trans. and comments. *Dante: oeuvres complètes*. Paris: Gallimard, Bibliothèque de la Pléiade, 1965.

----------. *Dante sous la pluie de feu*. Paris: Vrin, 1950.

Phàn Thi Ngoc Mai. *"La Chute" de Camus: le dernier testament*. Neuchâtel. Editions de la Bacconière, 1974.

Quillot, Roger. *La Mer et les prisons: essai sur Albert Camus*. Paris: Gallimard, 1956.

Sperber, M. A. "Camus's The Fall: the Icarus Complex." *American Imago*, 269-280.

Thompson, David B. "Dante's Ulysses and the Allegorical Journey." *Dante Studies*, 85 (1967), 35-58; rpt. in expanded form in *Dante's Epic Journeys*. Baltimore: n.p., 1974.

Dean Vasil

THE ETHICAL PRAGMATISM OF ALBERT CAMUS
Two Studies in the History of Ideas

American University Studies:
Series II, Romance Languages and Literature. Vol. 18
ISBN 0-8204-0166-8   XVI + 152 pp.   hardback US $ 21.85

In what, since the age of its Enlightenment, the West has perceived to be an absurd universe, it has had continually to choose between two ways of life as consequences of that perception and of the movement which gave it rise: these are the way of ethics and the way of modern historicist ideology, the way of a moral imperative without God and that of the will to become God in His place. The first is illogical, but the second is irrational, la «prédication de la surhumanité», as Camus says, «aboutissant à la fabrication méthodique des sous-hommes.» The way of ethics or of man as an end in himself is the way of Camus as well, and one the reflection of whose origins and *raison d'être* in his own thought is the subject of the two studies in the present essay.
Contents: Thought of Camus, Albert – Enlightenment and Existential Philosophy – Ethics and Pragmatism – History of Ideas in France and the Modern West.

PETER LANG PUBLISHING, INC.
34 East 39th Street
USA – New York, NY 10016